A Ghost of a Chance

A Ghost of a Chance

A Novel by
Joan Carris

Illustrated by Paul Henry

 Little, Brown and Company
Boston   Toronto   London

First Edition

The characters and events in this book are fictitious. Any similarity to real persons, living or dead, is coincidental and not intended by the author.

Library of Congress Cataloging-in-Publication Data

Carris, Joan Davenport.
  A ghost of a chance / Joan Carris.
    p.   cm.
    Summary: Punch and his friends spend a summer in North Carolina looking at dolphins, hunting for Blackbeard's buried treasure, and watching out for the famed pirate's ghost.
    ISBN 0-316-13016-8
    [1. Buried treasure—Fiction.   2. Blackbeard, d. 1718—Fiction.
    3. Pirates—Fiction.   4 Dolphins—Fiction.   5. Ghosts—Fiction.
    6.   North Carolina—Fiction.]   I. Title.
    PZ7.C2347Gh   1992
    [Fic]—dc20   91-29617

10 9 8 7 6 5 4 3 2 1

EB   MI

Published simultaneously in Canada
by Little, Brown & Company (Canada) Limited

Printed in the United States of America

Ghosts do exist: of this I have no doubt.
My files are too full of authenticated
documents and photographs to allow me to
believe anything to the contrary.

Raymond Lamont Brown
Phamtoms of the Sea, 1973

Acknowledgments

Thanks to the interest, patience, and delightful humor of JoAnne Powell, director of education at the North Carolina Maritime Museum in Beaufort, North Carolina, this book is accurate down to the last sea shell. A ton of gratitude, JoAnne.

And thanks also to the Duke University Marine Lab staff — for being there and doing such important work for so long and to the benefit of so many.

To M.D., the current owner of Hammock House, bless you for letting me spend so much time on your property. It was extremely thoughtful of you to be gone during August so that my characters could excavate your backyard.

A Ghost of a Chance

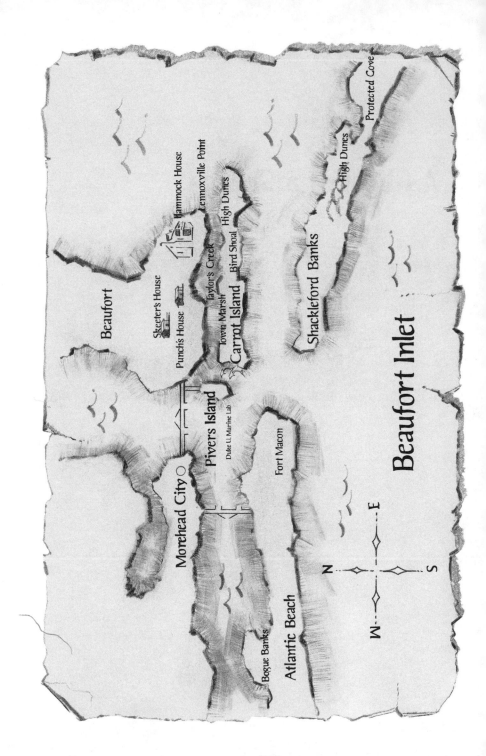

1•
Welcome to Beaufort

Punch Wagner was trying to be patient with his father. "We did it all," he said. "We unpacked, made the beds — we even put on suntan lotion. So can't we go?"

Right now! he wanted to holler. But he couldn't say why. His folks would think he was wacko.

"I see you're itching to leave," his father said, grunting as he raised the umbrella over the table on the outdoor deck. "But Lanky Grace is coming. His son will be your guide while we're here. I may have forgotten to mention that."

Punch looked at his friend Tom Ellis, who had come to North Carolina with the Wagners on vacation. Silently they shared their thoughts. Who wanted a strange kid hanging around? Especially now, when they had so much to plan.

"Dad!" cried Punch. "You're always telling me stuff when it's too late! This is really major and we didn't even know! We don't need a guide! We're *twelve*, remember?"

3

Professor Wagner peered over the top of his glasses. "Calm down, Philip, please. And give me credit for a little sense. Lanky Grace is one of the finest human beings on earth and I expect his son to be just like him. I'm trying to give you a lifelong friend and you're shouting at me."

Punch stared wordlessly at his father, Professor Siegfried Wagner. Patient, studious, musically gifted. Everything Punch was not. Why would he think he could select a best friend for his very different son? Punch nibbled at the inside of his cheek as he often did when he was upset.

Tom nudged him with an understanding elbow. "Come on," he said, "let's go check out the boat."

The screen door banged and Punch's sister, Lila, joined them. She was wearing a chartreuse bikini and sunglasses and was lugging her cello. "What a great place to practice," she announced, planting the spike of her cello in the deck.

"Yeah," breathed Tom, gazing dopily at Punch's sister.

Hoo-ee, thought Punch, wondering how many times in his life he would witness this scene. Both he and Lila had inherited their dad's red-gold hair and dark brown eyes, but while Punch had turned out nicely normal, Lila was just plain astounding. All males looked at her and lost their minds.

As Lila began tuning her cello, Punch urged Tom away from her, toward the steps that led down to the

4

boat dock. At the top of the steps they stopped to watch an approaching boat. In it were a man and a boy.

"Any Yankees here?" called the man, laughter in his voice.

"Lanky!" Punch's dad hurried across the deck and down the steps to the dock. There he hugged Mr. Grace, pulled back to grin at him, and hugged him again harder.

"You old crawdad!" he said. "Lord, it's been a long time. You look great. Haven't changed a bit."

Old crawdad? thought Punch. He couldn't remember when his dad had been as excited as now, ushering his old friend up the steps of their vacation house. At the top, Mr. Grace offered his hand to Punch.

Punch shook hands with the reed-slender man with hair like hay and eyes like aquamarines. In worn, sun-bleached clothes he appeared to drift rather than walk onto the deck.

"Welcome to North Carolina," he said, his accent immediately noticeable.

"Howdy," added his son, a younger double.

Straw people, Punch thought, remembering the enchanted brooms of *The Sorcerer's Apprentice* — picturing how each separate broomstraw had magically come to life. That was Lanky and his son. Big straw and little straw.

Mr. Grace said, "Thishere's Skeeter. He'll be in sixth grade come September. Skeeter?"

The boy's hand shot out. "Sir," he said, shaking

hands with Punch's father. He nodded at Punch and Tom but said nothing.

"Offer them a ride in the boat, son," prompted Mr. Grace. "They'd enjoy bein' out on the water."

"Yessir. Y'all wanta go out in the boat?"

Punch heard the boredom in Skeeter's voice. He wasn't any more interested in them than they were in him.

From the corner of the deck came Lila's voice. "If somebody said 'boat,' I can practice later. I'm about to croak in this heat." She set her cello aside and stood up.

Skeeter stared openly. "Yes, ma'am," he said with reverence. "I surely did say 'boat.'"

Lila giggled. "No one's ever called me ma'am. My name's Lila, okay?"

As Lila was being introduced to Mr. Grace, Punch's mom and their dog, Mozart, joined them on the deck. Mozart was a gray schnauzer who hated to be left out of anything. He barked off and on, just to be sociable, while everyone was talking.

Mrs. Wagner asked the Graces to stay for dinner. Punch's father told Skeeter he looked the same as his dad at age eleven. Mr. Grace recalled a camping trip he and Punch's father had taken to Shackleford Banks.

Punch grew sweaty and fidgety. "I'm going from rare to well done in this heat," he grumbled. "Let's get gone."

Skeeter nodded. Into the bubbling adult conversation he tossed "Bye, we're goin' in the boat."

Punch's mom stopped talking.

"You kids good swimmers?" Mr. Grace asked.

Mrs. Wagner answered for them. "Yes, they're excellent swimmers, but they're too young to just leap in a boat and take off. Sig Wagner, don't you look at me like that! Our kids have never done this and you know it."

Punch's dad put his arm around her. "I know, Dee, but Lanky and I went everywhere in that skiff, from the time we were ten. All the kids here do. A boat is the same as a bicycle here."

He paused, one of his eloquent conductor's hands arranging the few strands of hair atop his head. "Dee," he went on, "this's why we came here! So that Philip and Lila could do the things I did as a boy. Most of the places they'll go, the water's so shallow you can wade — and they won't do anything stupid. Lila's sixteen, after all, and Skeeter will watch out for them, won't you, Skeeter?"

"Yessir. I won't let 'em outa my sight."

Hunh! thought Punch, surprised and annoyed. Usually, Professor Wagner concerned himself only with Lila and her music schedule, leaving Punch and his activities in the care of his mother, who understood kids and their needs.

Only my dad, Punch fumed, would think a sixth-grader should be in charge here! But he'd go along with anything now, just to get away.

"Mom," he said, "Dad's right. We won't do anything dumb, but we need to get going. Night is falling!"

Mr. Grace smiled at Punch. "Y'all have fun. Skeeter, beach the boat for swimmin', hear? No leapin' in and outa the boat. And don't be gone too long this first time."

Nobody waited for any more discussion. They pounded down the steps to the dock and the boat. Lila sat in the bow, Punch and Tom on the middle seat, and Skeeter in the stern beside the outboard motor.

The Graces' boat was a flat-bottomed, wooden fishing skiff that maneuvered easily through the shallow inlets and shoals around Beaufort. It had a ripe, fishy smell and was equipped with poles, a gill net, a clam rake, and a fish box. Punch was about to ask if they could go fishing when Skeeter revved the engine, killing any chance for talk.

After only a few seconds, Lila made motions at Skeeter. When he slowed the motor she asked, "Is that Carrot Island?"

"Yes, ma'am."

"Forget the 'ma'am,' " she said. "It makes me feel ninety-four. But I would like a real tourist lecture, okay?" She gave him an incandescent smile.

Skeeter thawed visibly. "Okay, Lila." He sat tall, thought a second, then began. "This's an inland waterway called Taylor's Creek. It's got a nice deep channel for yachts. We get million-dollar boats here, Lord's truth."

Just outside the waterway's "No Wake" zone, he revved the engine again and pointed them west out of Beaufort Harbor on the way to Beaufort Inlet.

"Up ahead," Skeeter hollered over the engine, "that's Pivers Island. It's got a national fisheries lab and the Duke University Marine Lab. I'm over thar all the time. Duke runs a year-round dolphin watch and I help."

Dolphin watch? Punch had been wondering how to enlist Skeeter's help with their incredible idea, but the word *dolphin* made him forget. To him, dolphins were the most special of all wild things. A dolphin poster covered the wall above his bed at home and another was taped to his closet door. Three dolphin sculptures sat atop his bookcase.

"How do you run a dolphin watch?" he shouted.

"By payin' attention," Skeeter yelled back. He frowned at the motor and slowed it down before he resumed. "A dolphin's one a the most complex mammals alive, but you hafta be around 'em regular to figure that out."

Oh, brother, thought Punch. This kid has to be the biggest know-it-all I ever met.

Skeeter continued relentlessly. "You gotta take good care a dolphins. I check 'em all the time and if one's sick or in trouble, I tell the professors."

Impressed in spite of the boy's manner, Punch nodded at the marine laboratory and said, "Are you going to work there when you grow up?"

The slender face darkened. "You funnin' me? How'm I gonna do that?" He turned away and speeded up the motor, separating himself from them with its steady noise.

Lila made a face at Punch and shrugged her shoulders. How could you know? her gestures said.

Hurt and angry, Punch shook his head. What was Skeeter's problem, anyway? But then he thought, Why do I care? I just met him.

Before long Skeeter cut the engine and pointed. One gray dorsal fin showed. A long gray body followed. More fins and rippling water told him it was an entire school.

Punch exchanged joyful glances with Tom and Lila. He had never been this close to his favorite wild creature.

Three dolphins rose upward in unison, a glistening, silver arc of perfection. At the top of the arc, they curved down and entered the water simultaneously.

"Just like Sea World!" Tom called out.

"If you want 'em to come over here, you can't make a lotta noise," Skeeter warned.

"Sorry," Tom said. "You mean they'll come close?"

"They know me. I swim with 'em lotsa times. Only don't you tell Daddy that."

He swims with them! The words planted themselves in Punch's brain as the dolphins came nearer and

10

nearer. Only a few yards off the bow, a pair of smaller dolphins leapt upward in tandem, their natural smiles in place.

Punch stopped thinking altogether. He sat motionless, surrounded by dolphins carving lines of beauty in the air. He watched and worshiped.

One small dolphin approached and Punch held his breath.

"She's just a coupla years old," whispered Skeeter."Isn't she a love?" He made a sweet, whistling sound.

The laughing dolphin raised her head and squeaked an answer, then swam straight to Skeeter's hand. "Hey, Sweetheart," he crooned, fondling her head with both hands. She opened her mouth and let him rub her tongue and gums.

That's just how I'd do it, Punch thought . . . if I could. He was drawn to this new Skeeter, and he envied him so strongly it was almost a physical pain.

When Skeeter sat back in his seat, Sweetheart glided to the bow, where she stopped to eye Lila.

"Reach out your hand real slow," prompted Skeeter.

"She won't gnaw on it or anything, will she?"

The boys hooted with laughter and Lila turned red. "Okay, okay," she said, leaning forward to touch Sweetheart's head. She patted gingerly, with only a few fingers.

Sweetheart sensed Lila's lack of interest and left her for Punch's hand, eagerly outstretched over the water.

11

Punch felt the cool gray skin slide under his fingers — how she felt both firm and soft. One dolphin eye examined him, looking directly into his own eyes.

The she flipped away, diving under the boat, coming up right into Tom's hands.

"She likes us," Tom said softly. "She wants us to pet her, doesn't she?"

"Acourse she does. Dolphins aren't afraid a people, not much, anyhow, and they love to play. See? Her family's comin' now. Purely amazin', they are," Skeeter concluded.

Hard feelings were forgotten in the warm, pink evening as the dolphins entertained them with play that was half circus, half marine ballet. They sprang upward in twos and threes for the joy of leaping. They zoomed in for caresses, then flipped away, swimming round and round the boat in silver circles. By the time they left, squeaking and whistling to one another, Punch knew their names and had petted them all.

Also, he had made a decision. He was going to swim with them. He just had to. He could imagine how much fun it would be, almost like being a dolphin.

As Skeeter started the engine, Punch leaned back to talk to him. "I'll be very careful and do whatever you say, but the next time you swim with them, I want to, too, okay?"

Skeeter became very still. "No, it's not okay," he said. "Nobody's supposed to swim with 'em unless

thar's a reason. A real good scientific reason. *They aren't toys!"*

With a vicious twist of the wrist he revved the motor until it screamed, shooting the skiff forward so that Punch lurched dangerously backward. He gripped the boat for safety as did Tom and his sister.

And now, Punch longed to haul off and slug this kid. It was okay for *him* to swim with the dolphins — just nobody else. I've never met anyone so touchy and unpredictable, Punch thought. I sure wish Dad could see how me and my new lifelong friend are getting along.

Bathed in noise and anger, they turned south, around the western end of Carrot Island. Lila waved at Skeeter and pointed to the island.

Skeeter cut back the engine and waited.

"Can we go swimming there? I love those little beaches, and I think I saw horses." She smiled at Skeeter, who said nothing.

"Come on," Lila pleaded. "I did see horses, didn't I?"

Under her gaze Skeeter caved in. "Yes, ma'am. Those're wild horses, though, so you can't go up to 'em.

"I guess we can stop here," he went on. "We'll go up yonder toward Bird Shoal and y'all can hunt for sand dollars. Tourists just love sand dollars."

The way he said *tourists* set Punch's teeth on edge. As they pulled the skiff onto the beach, he told Skeeter, "You don't really have to show us around. We'll be in *seventh grade* in a few weeks, you know. We can make it on our own."

Skeeter's sea-blue eyes appraised him coolly. When he answered, his voice held no emotion at all. "Y'all can do more stuff and better stuff with me than without me. And if I'm showin' y'all around, I don't have to work. I'm mortal tired a workin' on this job Daddy's got now."

"Job?" Punch asked. He didn't know anyone eleven years old who had to work.

"Acourse," said Skeeter. "Daddy's trainin' me to be a carpenter. He's the best in all Carteret County."

"That's terrific," Lila said, moving to stand beside him. "But now you get a vacation just like us. Come on, you can help me look for sand dollars."

Skeeter went with her readily. Punch and Tom waded into the water. "Could be the world's all-time longest vacation with that kid," Punch said.

Tom started to answer and yelped instead. "Hey! I just stepped on a sand dollar — and here's a sea olive!"

In time, the absolute perfection of the place washed away the anger. All four of them raced and floated and dove and stood on their hands, legs quivering as the waves threatened to topple them. Only when they were exhausted did they lie down in the shallows.

Overhead, in the bluest sky Punch had ever seen, circled the questing, calling sea gulls. A gull's piercing cry always made him feel sad. He didn't tell anyone that, of course, but he decided to keep bread in his pockets for them.

He lay still, eyes closed, and let the water lap over his body. He hadn't been on an island before, but it was definitely one of the world's finest places to be. "So," he said lazily, "what do you guys do here for fun?"

"Well," Skeeter replied, "sometimes we watch movies at Wally's place. His mama's got a real good job and they've got a VCR. But movies cost a pile a money. I reckon we fish, mostly. Dig clams. Slap bugs. We slap bugs a lot."

Punch laughed. Skeeter could be funny when he wanted. Maybe now they would get along better.

Just then the incredible idea he and Tom had had earlier popped back into his mind.

"Hey!" he said, excited anew. "Blackbeard's house! Let's go there, okay?" During the seemingly endless car ride that day, he had read one of his father's books on Beaufort and been astounded to learn that Blackbeard had lived there.

"Nah, we can't go thar. That house is haunted."

"No lie?" Punch sat upright, a layer of sand oozing wetly down his back.

"Awesome," Tom said. "I've never been in a real haunted house. He hid a ton of treasure, too, and nobody's ever found it. He's the world's all-time greatest pirate."

Lila fixed her dark brown eyes on Tom. Each word encased in ice, she said, "You've got to be kidding."

16

Tom just looked at her.

"He was a total creep!" She sat up and looked down at Tom, a rare sharpness in her voice. "He murdered people all over the place and he *used* women like — like —"

Skeeter put a slender hand on her flailing arm. "He's dead now, Lila. They trapped him up near Ocracoke and stabbed him ever which way. Cut his head off and evertheng. He's real dead."

"Good," said Punch. "So we can go to his house."

Skeeter shook his head. "Somebody owns it now. Anyhow, Blackbeard's spirit isn't dead."

Lila wrapped her arms around her legs. "I'll bet you're right," she said. Lila read horror stories all the time and considered herself an expert on the supernatural.

Punch could hardly believe his luck. A real haunted house! Pots of pirate treasure! And dolphins, too. How his father could have failed to mention these astonishing facts was beyond him.

To Tom he said, "We'll check out his house tomorrow morning, first thing. The treasure could still be there."

"Y'all are crazy!" Skeeter said. "That house is haunted for sure! If you even thenk you're goin' thar, you better tell me what kind a funeral you want. Y'all like happy music or sad? Flowers or a donation to your favorite charity? Just let me know."

2•
Even Mozart Says No

"I know it sounds wacko," Punch said to Tom as they lay in their beds that night. "But somebody's going to find that treasure, so why not us?"

"I guess," Tom said, yawning as he rolled over. "Tons of people have looked, though, so we should forget his house. It's too obvious."

"That's why we have to look there! It's so obvious, nobody'd think he'd put it there. So he did! He was a very smart pirate. He'd want it handy. His very own bank, see? Let's go first thing tomorrow."

No response came from Tom's bed. He's asleep, Punch decided. It figures. He thought of the long day they'd had and the awkward evening with Skeeter.

Skeeter Grace. The straw boy. He was like everything else on this vacation — different. Punch was still stinging from the curt lecture about swimming with the dolphins. "Must think he owns them," Punch muttered into his pillow. Whenever he thought of Skeeter's words, *"They're not toys,"* he got angry all over again.

"I know that!" he said out loud.

"Rrarf?" Mozart raised his head off the bed.

"Sorry, Mozie." Punch patted the warm, alert head and curled around his dog as he did every night. Dogs are nicer than most people, he thought. I bet dolphins are a lot like dogs, only smarter.

He remembered the look and feel and sound of the dolphins all around him, only hours ago. Imagining what it would be like to swim with them would never be good enough. Not anymore. Some warm, pink evening like tonight, no matter what Skeeter said, he was going to swim with those dolphins.

At breakfast the next day Punch's mom said, "Folks, this is one Monday I plan to spend as a vegetable. I'll do anything you want tomorrow."

"Sounds good," said his dad. "Tonight Lanky and I are going fishing. You're all welcome to join us."

"I'm practicing this morning," Lila said, serious about keeping her place in the New Jersey State Orchestra. "Later, the kids I met in town last night are coming here."

Punch listened, overjoyed to hear everyone's plans. Now he and Tom could easily slip away to Blackbeard's house. "We're going to check out Beaufort," he said as they started for the front door.

"Better wait for Skeeter," said Professor Wagner.

"Why? He's not our keeper!" With a click, Punch snapped the leash onto Mozart's collar.

His dad frowned. "Don't be so touchy, Philip."

"Touchy?" squeaked Punch, his voice making an unplanned swoop upward. "You ought to hang around Skeeter!"

"Really? I'm surprised. Give me an example, please."

Punch flopped down on the couch. "Okay. Yesterday he was bragging about how he helped the Duke marine lab with its dolphin watch, so I asked if he was going to work there when he grew up. He really chewed me out! And there were other times. I mean, we're talking picky here!"

"Yeah," said Tom. "It doesn't take much."

"Hmm," mused Professor Wagner. "That lab is staffed with college professors, of course." He sat down beside Punch. "No one in Skeeter's family has ever been to college. I tried to talk Lanky into going when we were teenagers, but he loved carpentry so much he wasn't interested. Also, the Graces have very little money."

Mrs. Wagner joined in. "Maybe Skeeter'd like to work at the lab and knows he can't. Do you think that's it, Punch?"

He shrugged. "Maybe. But I'm not asking him, no way. Being told off once is plenty, thanks."

Punch's dad leaned back against the couch, hands behind his head. "Let's be patient. After all, we just got here. And you've already met the dolphins. I knew you'd like that."

"Sure!" Punch hesitated, then said, "Dad, why didn't you tell me about the dolphins? You never tell me the big, important stuff!"

"I don't need to give you a preview of everything, Punch. You have a good mind of your own, and I'd rather you met life spontaneously."

He patted his son's shoulder. "I'll tell you about the small, important things. Those are the ones you need to be aware of beforehand."

"Oh," Punch said, knowing he'd have to think this out later. It was pretty heavy for vacation.

"I guess we'll be waiting outside then," Punch replied. "Somewhere on Front Street. We're taking Mozie, so Skeeter can't miss us. Mozie barks at all the sea gulls."

He and Tom and Mozart left the house and headed down the front sidewalk. Lila followed shortly after. "You guys still planning to go to Blackbeard's house?" she asked.

"Yup," Punch said. "And Skeeter better not blab it around, either. He acts like he owns this place!"

"Well, he has lived here all his life," she said. "If a mess of tourists piled into my little town every summer, I'd hate it." She waited, expectant. "So. Are you guys going to tell me what's going on or not? I won't talk."

Punch looked at Tom. Tom gave a tiny nod of agreement. "Okay," Punch said, looking around to make sure no one could overhear, "we're going to find Blackbeard's treasure."

"Today?" she asked, teasing. Then, soberly, "I'll bet that house is some kind of historic property. Be careful what you do around there. Where is it, anyway?"

Mozart began pulling on his leash and Punch followed. "It's called Hammock House and it's only a few blocks from here. I checked the map Mr. Grace brought us. But don't tell Mom and Dad, and quit giving us orders."

Lila waggled her fingers good-bye. "Nice having you around for a few, brief years. That could be a real haunted house, you know." She turned and went indoors.

"She thinks we're crazy," Tom said.

"They said Columbus was crazy, too." Punch began walking and Mozart trotted gladly forward. "And Admiral Peary and the Wright brothers and Ponce de Leon —"

"They were right about Poncy," inserted Tom.

"Okay, so there isn't a fountain of youth. But we know there's treasure!" The thought of it made him walk faster.

"Hey!" came a voice. "Y'all are supposed to wait for me!"

Punch told himself to be cool. I am *not touchy*, he repeated silently while they waited for Skeeter.

"Y'all are goin' whar?" cried Skeeter when he heard.

"You know," Punch said, turning left on Fulford Street. "See?" he announced. "Hammock Lane up on the right."

Slowly, as if he were speaking to dimwits, Skeeter said, "That . . . house . . . is . . . haunted." He plowed his straw-colored hair with a nervous hand. "Tourists get all worked up over Blackbeard and I'll never know why. That treasure's been gone so long it's hopeless. This's purely crazy!"

"The magic word," muttered Punch. And the kid had called him a tourist again. But I am cool, he reminded himself. I am not touchy.

"Look, you guys," he said, wishing they could understand how he felt, "forget about ghosts. Think about the treasure. What if we did find it? Think!"

Under the burning August sun, the three of them stood at the corner of Hammock Lane and thought of pirate treasure.

Tom said, "I guess I'd buy a Porsche. A red one."

"My Lamborghini'll beat your Porsche," said Punch.

Skeeter giggled.

"So?" Tom asked. "What're you going to get?"

Skeeter shrugged. "Don't need a car. I go everwhar in the boat. New boat'd be nice, though."

But there is something he really, really wants, Punch thought, nearly blurting it out. It was much more important than a car. Punch didn't need another of Skeeter's lectures, however, and so he said nothing. When he thinks of it, Punch decided, he'll hunt for sure.

Mozart yanked on his leash, and again they went forward. Skeeter walked with them only a few yards, then pointed across the narrow street. "That's it," he said.

Punch and Tom stared at the square, two-story house glistening whitely in the hot sun. The two chimneys, the front porches — one above the other — and the trim were all stark, staring white.

"Hunh," Punch observed. "Doesn't look haunted to me."

"Me either," said Tom. "Those bushes are nice."

"That's just yaupon," Skeeter said. "Grows all over. You can make tea outa yaupon leaves. Hey! Whar's he goin'?"

They watched as Mozart crawled into the shade of the yaupon hedge.

"Get him back!" cried Skeeter.

"You really think it's haunted, don't you?" Punch asked.

"I know it is! My friend Wally heard that poor French girl screamin' and screamin' one time. He won't even come on this street, nossir."

"What French girl?" chorused Punch and Tom.

"I reckoned you didn't know. And it's history, not some legend or made-up story."

"So tell us," urged Punch.

"I'm gettin' to it. Just calm yourself." He frowned at Hammock House for several seconds before he began. "See, Blackbeard decided he wanted this real fancy French ship. I guess it had a whole pile a loot on board and some rich folks from Europe.

24

"Well, he and his men outran her and boarded her and just went wild with those big cutlasses — killed all kinds a folks. Blackbeard made everbody walk the plank that wasn't already dead, except for this real pretty girl. He took her for himself, know what I mean?"

Punch and Tom nodded.

"He brought her here and she couldn't stand it, poor theng. She screamed and screamed. So he got right disgusted with her and took her out behind the house and had his men to hang her from a live oak tree and bury her right thar on the spot. But she's *still screamin'*, Lord's truth."

Punch and Tom looked at each other and nodded. "That's a ghost all right," Punch said. "A murder victim won't rest till justice is done."

Skeeter's head bobbed up and down in a satisfied manner. "You got that right, so let's get on outa here."

"No way," Punch said, louder than he intended. He was boiling hot and tired of doing nothing. "I came here to look around." He walked across the sunny front yard to where Mozart lay panting in the shade of the hedge.

Tom started to follow but stopped when Skeeter called out. "I'm only waitin' a coupla minutes. Y'all watch out for Blackbeard!" He sat down in the grass, a small doom prophet, stiffly erect.

Punch whirled around. "Blackbeard, too, hunh? Geez, it's a regular ghost party!" He shook his head

25

derisively and bent down to pick up Mozart's leash before continuing toward the back of the house.

Skeeter colored with anger. "Some folks haven't got the sense God gave a baby chicken, just like Mamaw says." He glared at Punch's back a second before going on. "The bottom a that house is made a ballast stone. Came here in ships, long time ago. Spirits stay in stone. 'Specially bad spirits like his."

Tom sucked in his breath. "I wish you hadn't said that. Lila told us that, too, hunh, Punch?"

"Yup." Punch lifted Mozart over a low fence between the front and back yards. He hopped over himself and stood still, staring at Tom. In spite of what he had said to Skeeter, he hoped he wouldn't have to examine the backyard all alone.

Tom's eyes went from Punch to Skeeter, sitting across the street, and back to Punch. "Man, this better be okay," he said, moving toward the fence.

In the yard behind Hammock House there was no sun, only the deep shade that tall, old oaks provide. Several spiky, overgrown plants edged the property, but no flowers brightened the gloom. Here, it felt strangely cold.

Punch gripped Mozart's leash, but he needn't have. Mozart was not sallying forth to sniff the new yard. He was glued to Punch's left side as if he were a perfectly trained dog, which he was not.

"Okay. Here we are," Punch announced.

Tom looked at the impressive old oaks. "Wonder which tree they hanged her from?"

"Don't think about that! Check out the house. It looks all closed up." Punch fervently hoped it was. He didn't know what the local laws were about trespassing, but he was pretty sure they were doing it.

Tom stared at the closed-in back porch and shifted from one foot to the other. "With colored panes in those windows, we can't tell if anybody's in there or not. But I don't like it here. We can't dig here, anyway, remember? Skeeter said somebody owns it now."

"But it's the most logical place!"

Still, Blackbeard's property felt dark and alien — set apart somehow, and not just by being the oldest house in town. A vision of the pirate himself was vivid in Punch's mind. He could see him here, striding among these trees, his heavy black beard matted with blood and greasy food, a smile on his face as he watched his men hang the pretty girl who refused to submit, who kept on screaming and —

Something plopped onto the roof at the back of the house. It tumbled across the shingles, dropped to the ground, and rolled to within a few feet of the boys.

Both of them jumped backward.

"Heh, heh," Punch laughed, embarrassed. He made himself pick up the thing that had scared them. I am cool, he repeated silently. And this is some kind of joke. He held out the small object for Tom to see.

"Look, it's just a toy, probably from a gumball machine." Despite his brave talk, Punch's stomach knotted as he stared at the thing on his palm. It was a tiny plastic skull with red eyes that glittered at him.

"It's a warning," Tom said, backing away. "Somebody knows we're looking for the treasure. Somebody wants us to go away."

"Ah, come on! It's Skeeter, trying to scare us."

"Yeah, and it worked. I'm going."

Mozart followed Tom. "See?" Tom told Punch. "Even Mozart knows."

When he had gone the length of his leash, Mozart halted. He whimpered and pulled toward Tom and the front yard.

Reluctantly, Punch yielded. He was disgusted with himself for giving in, but maybe Tom and Mozart and Skeeter were right and this wasn't the place to hunt after all.

When he got to the front of the house, he saw Tom standing on the sidewalk, an odd expression on his face.

"You still think Skeeter threw that skull?" Tom asked, pointing to Skeeter's spot on the grass.

It was empty.

3•
The Search Begins

"There'll be better places to hunt," said Tom, visibly happier as they left Hammock House behind.

"Well, maybe," Punch replied. At the corner he turned to look back at Blackbeard's house. He had been so sure it was the right place. Scary, yes, but that was probably to be expected. Hunting for pirate treasure wasn't supposed to be easy. Otherwise everybody'd be doing it.

"We could go to the library and make a list of places," Tom suggested.

"Yeah," Punch said, and then added as they neared their house, "First, let's get that book Dad had in the car."

A note on the table said that Punch's parents were on a walk. He could hear Lila sawing away on her cello out on the deck. Punch found the book and took it to the kitchen, where Tom was fixing a snack.

Minutes later they both exclaimed, "A tunnel!" as they read the history of Blackbeard's house.

In the 1700s, Hammock House had been situated

on raised ground — a hummock or hammock, from which it got its name — right on Taylor's Creek. From the water to the house wound the secret tunnel, which was now closed up, according to the author. Carrot Island, then called Cart Island, was only a short row away. Long ago, Blackbeard had tied up to his house at high tide.

"Cool," murmured Punch, studying an artist's drawing of Hammock House in Blackbeard's day. He liked it better then. Now, many feet of additional land separated the house from the water, and the wonderful tunnel was no more.

He looked out the big picture window at the oldest portion of Carrot Island, the eastern end across the water from the pirate's house. It was such an obvious place to bury treasure that no one would expect him to choose it. Perhaps that was how he had outsmarted the world.

"Should we check out Carrot Island first?" he asked.

"Mmff," Tom said around a large mouthful of sandwich. He swallowed hastily. "Sure. We have to do the logical stuff. If somebody found treasure there and we hadn't even checked, we'd feel really dumb."

"Right." Punch's excitement for the hunt bloomed again. The library search for likely places could wait. "There's a tool shed under the deck," he said. "I'll get spades."

On his way across the deck, he made a face at his

sister, who was seated in the shade practicing her cello. "See? The ghost didn't get us!" he shouted over her music. He figured she didn't need to know about the little skull.

Lila saluted him with her bow and looked genuinely happy to see him. It was no good getting angry or even trying to argue with Lila. She was too nice.

He was feeling around for a light in the dimness of the shed when a voice behind him said, "Whatcha doin'?"

Punch jerked upright and whammed his head on a ceiling beam in the low shed. Bone met wood with a loud thump.

"Oh, I am so sorry," Skeeter said with elaborate politeness. "I didn't mean to scare y'all."

"You didn't scare me!" yelled Punch, rubbing the painful lump on his head. He backed out of the shed and glared at Skeeter. "What're you doing here?"

"I'm your guide, remember?"

Hah! Punch thought. Little know-it-all. Little sixth-grade smarty-pants. Just because you happen to live down here and we don't —

Some of his incredible anger must have showed on his face for Skeeter said again, in a different voice, "I really am sorry. Let's get an ice cube for that bump."

Punch stomped into the house behind him. He put an ice cube on his throbbing head and didn't even look in Skeeter's direction.

Tom-the-peacemaker explained what he and Punch were planning. He finished with "I suppose the whole world has dug up that island, huh?"

"Lord's truth," Skeeter said with feeling. "But I'll take you thar if you want."

Don't strain yourself, son, Punch thought. We'd much rather go without you. His anger deepened as he realized they couldn't go at all without Skeeter and his boat. His parents would never trust him to take their rented one.

Tom got two spades from the well-stocked shed while Punch smoldered in silence. The lump on his head felt as big as a cereal bowl and he was sick of trying to get along with Skeeter.

By now, the comforting ice cube had become a dripping morsel. As he stepped into the skiff, Punch hurled it into the water. A few gulls swooped low where it splashed, then wheeled up and away with disappointed cries.

"Come back!" he called, digging in his pockets. "Here!" He tore off bits of toast and tossed them at the gulls.

"It's cracked wheat," he called as he stood in the bow. "Very good for you!" As the gulls saw him and swiftly found his bread, Punch began to feel better.

Then he heard snickering. "Y'all don't need to sell it. A gull'll eat anytheng."

"I know that!" snapped Punch. "Can't you tell when somebody's making a joke?"

"Hey, guys," begged Tom. "Come on." Then, changing the subject he said, "What's that, Skeeter?"

Skeeter had picked up a pole from the floor of the boat. It had a handle on one end and a round disk on the other. "Metal detector," he said, holding it up. "Handy, huh?"

Punch couldn't believe it. A real metal detector? Right here in the boat?

"How's come you've got that?" he demanded.

"Lots of us got'em. Tourists lose all kinds a money in the sand over at Atlantic Beach. After a nice sunny weekend, I can find five, six dollars."

So we tourists have our uses, Punch thought bitterly.

Tom pounded the seat of the boat. "Awesome! That'll make treasure hunting a snap."

Punch agreed, though he'd never give Skeeter the satisfaction of saying so. To himself he sang, "Pieces of eight, pieces of eight!" Aloud he said, "So let's go."

"Which part of the island you aimin' for?" Skeeter asked, tugging at the cord on the outboard engine.

"Old parts," Punch replied. "Parts that might have been here when Blackbeard was. We need to look for real old tree stumps — stuff like that."

On the way across Taylor's Creek, Punch hefted the metal detector and examined its dishlike end. "How far down can it find something metal?" he asked.

"This's a real good one," Skeeter said. "It'll find a coin six, seven inches down."

"That's *all*?" Punch could almost hear the crash

33

landing of his soaring hopes. "He'd never put it in a dinky little hole like that!"

"Y'all should just forget Blackbeard's treasure," Skeeter said. "But you could get lucky out here and find some extra change with this baby." He patted his detector as if it were a friendly bloodhound.

The skiff scraped the sands a few feet offshore at Carrot Island. "Hop out and we'll beach her," Skeeter said.

"Forget it," said Punch. "This's a waste of time."

Skeeter insisted on securing the boat anyway. Then all three sat glumly on the beach, looking across the island. Thickets of shrubs and low trees dotted this eastern end. Behind one dense thicket, things were moving.

"Wild horses," Skeeter whispered. "Set still, hear?"

The horses munched their way around the thicket. The lead pony, a brown male with a black mane, snorted and rolled his eyes when he noticed the boys. He waited until he saw how still they were before taking his harem into the open.

Punch was intrigued by the small, scruffy horses, clearly wild and dependent on nature. Like little Misty of Chincoteague, he thought, remembering a book he had read a few years ago.

He turned his thoughts back to the problem of pirate treasure. By the time the horses ambled behind a cedar thicket, he had an idea. "Let's dig first, then use the detector," he suggested to Tom. "Come on, we'll find the old places on the island and start there."

"Y'all better get at it," Skeeter said. "Time's wastin' and I'm the cook tonight. Daddy'll be late."

"Does your mom work nights?" Punch asked. He handed one spade to Tom and took the other.

"I don't have a momma. She ran off when I was a baby."

Punch stared at Skeeter. He had spoken with no emotion whatever — as if to say, "Oh, we don't have a pet." Punch couldn't imagine life without his mom. He certainly couldn't picture her running away and leaving her family.

"I'm sorry," he said, looking right at Skeeter.

"Never mind. Me and Daddy are just like that," he said, holding up two fingers tight together. "Mamaw and Papaw live close by, so I get more motherin' than I can do with sometimes."

"Mamaw and Papaw?"

"I'll bet y'all say Gramma and Grampa."

"Oh, yeah." Punch was annoyed with himself for asking before he thought about it. Of course, the North Carolina Know-It-All had understood right away.

"How about here?" Tom suggested, tamping the ground. "See that big old stump? Looks right to me."

Punch checked all four directions and agreed that this was a likely place. They began digging and occasionally Skeeter tested spots with the metal detector. Mainly Skeeter lay on his back and watched the clouds.

"What'll it do" — Punch grunted as he heaved a load of sand out of the hole — "when it finds metal?"

"It'll beep. The louder it beeps, the smilier we get."

Hmm, 'smilier,' Punch thought. It's a whole new language down here.

Several strenuous minutes passed. Punch and Tom, who had been merely hot before, now poured sweat, which drew stinging gnats and hungry mosquitoes.

When they were over two feet down and the hole was many feet in diameter, Punch stopped. "Okay, test all across the bottom," he ordered. Panting, he and Tom lay down in the shade and scratched their insect bites.

"Don't count on anything," Tom warned.

Skeeter proved him right in seconds. "Nothin' in here. Gotta fill this in and dig another one. This is nature reserve. You gotta leave it the way you found it."

Punch stiffened, hating Skeeter's bossy tone. He knew this area was in the Rachel Carson Estuary system. He had read that and paid little attention.

Punch made himself remember what he was hunting for — how glorious it would be to discover gold plates, buckets of precious gems, silver cups and trays. "Okeydokey!" he said, springing to his feet. We'll see who's tough here, he thought. I'm not just any old tourist, no way.

Six more times, in six promising locations, he and Tom dug huge holes, tested them, and filled them back in. They found a few old, small bottles of brown and green glass while they were digging and two rusted pieces of metal that might have been anything — except pieces of eight.

"Museum'll wanta see those bottles," Skeeter said.

"Whoopee," replied Punch as he scratched a mammoth swollen bite on his leg.

"This's just the first day." Tom's voice was hearty.

"Mister Psychologist," said Punch. "Tomorrow we bring bug repellent and a lot of lunch."

Skeeter plopped down on the sand nearby. Perky and rested because he hadn't lifted one spadeful, he grinned at them. "Y'all sure are stubborn. I don't thenk a coupla cars is worth all this."

Punch almost told him off. Almost. Just in time he remembered that he was cool. He was not touchy like Skeeter.

Punch heaved himself up off the sand and put his spade into the boat. When he turned to Skeeter, he kept his voice calm — old and patient-sounding. "It's more than cars. A lot more. You should be digging, too. You've got a real good reason to hunt for treasure."

"What do y'all mean by that?"

"Don't get mad. Just think about it, okay?" Punch dove into the water, more grateful for its soothing coolness than he could ever remember being.

4•
When Two Became Three

"You think Skeeter'll come back tomorrow?" Tom asked, wincing as he flexed his arm muscles. "We could use some help digging." He and Punch were upstairs changing into clean clothes before dinner.

"Well, he's the one who needs money," Punch replied. "We don't, not really. It'd just be so cool to find it! I bet they'd interview us for all kinds of stuff — papers, magazines. Heck, yeah."

He socked Tom happily. "TV programs, movies! We *really could find it,* you know. Weirder things have happened."

"Mmhmm," Tom said. "Like little skulls falling out of the sky."

"Punch? Tom? Dinner's been ready for five minutes," Mrs. Wagner called from the bottom of the stairs.

At the table, Punch was careful to tell his mom how good dinner tasted. In the Graces' house, Skeeter was cooking. Ugh. Vacuuming or carrying out the trash was okay, but Punch hated cooking. Things went seriously wrong for no good reason every time he tried it. He counted on his mom for food — and for many other things. He hoped she was happy and never even thought of running away.

As they ate, Punch's dad said, "No fishing tonight, folks, sorry. Lanky forgot that he'd promised extra time to his builder. Seems to me he puts in awfully long hours."

"And there's nobody to help," Punch said, salting his baked potato. "Mrs. Grace ran away when Skeeter was a baby. How could she do that?"

The professor's face was somber. "No one knows, Philip, but Lanky deserved much better."

Lila put her hand on her father's. "He's awfully nice, Dad. So's Skeeter."

Oh, yeah? Punch gave his sister a disgusted look.

"One of the kids I met last night," Lila was saying, "has a job with Mr. Grace's builder. Remember meeting Johnny Keith this afternoon, Dad? He's the cute one — the one with the guitar."

"I remember the guitar. But Lila, dear, how did you meet those kids? We've only been here a day and a half."

"Dad, she's like flypaper," Punch said.

Lila frowned across the table. "That's gross!"

"Philip, really!" cried his mother.

His dad gazed thoughtfully at Punch's sister, who

tonight was breathtaking in emerald green. "I see what he means, Lila. Boys are attracted to you, and once they know you they are stuck because you're so sweet."

She made a face. "Ooh, that's a bit thick, Dad, don't you think?"

"No," he said, considering her. "Not at all."

Punch saw the moony expression on Tom's face and changed the subject. "Hey, Dad, do they have sea horses here? I think I saw one today in some water weeds."

His father leaned toward him. "Yes. And congratulations. They're hard to spot. I used to find them in seagrass beds, hanging on to the algae with their tails. I was awfully good at finding them," he said. "My parents tried and never could."

He turned to Lila. "Well, shall I get out my violin and we'll have a little concert, since we can't go fishing?"

"Tomorrow, maybe," Lila said. "Those kids are coming tonight to take me into town to check out the music. You know, on the docks."

He nodded gloomily. "I know."

"Poor Sig. No partner," teased Punch's mom. "Let's get out those games we brought. I haven't played Boggle in ages and we all like that."

The boys forced themselves to stay awake for a few games, but it wasn't easy. Even in sand, digging for treasure had been extremely hard work.

It would build huge muscles, though. I might make

the junior high football team as a seventh-grader, Punch thought. Tom had always been big and strong, perfect linebacker material. And I'm fast, he thought. An end maybe? I'll be in shape for the very first practice.

Early Tuesday morning Skeeter appeared on the Wagners' deck. Punch knew there was trouble as soon as he saw the slender, set face.

He misunderstood what I said, Punch decided. How can I explain without hurting his feelings or getting into a big, fat argument?

"So, how's it going?" Punch asked. He gnawed on the interior of his cheek with some anxiety.

"It's not. I'm gonna work with Daddy today. No point in wastin' any more time —"

"Skeeter!" said Mrs. Wagner, coming out to the deck from the kitchen. "I tried to call your house earlier but you both had left. Will you see your dad today so you can remind him you two are eating here this evening?"

"I'll see him," Skeeter said.

"No you won't," Punch said. He had had it with this kid running the show. I may be just a crummy tourist, he thought, but I'm not a total idiot. Skeeter needs to hunt for treasure even if he doesn't know it.

With an odd mix of emotions roiling inside him, Punch bounced up from his seat and stood next to Skeeter. "We're going back to Carrot Island," he said with a gusto that astonished even him. "Skeeter's taking us. We haven't dug for clams yet . . . lots of stuff."

Punch held his breath, gambling that Skeeter would rather be with them than with his father and the carpentry he hated.

Skeeter's aqua eyes were glacial chips, but he said nothing.

"Hurry up, Tom!" Punch chirruped, eager to escape before Skeeter decided to protest.

"Okay," said Punch's mom, "but this is a family vacation. We want you guys to do things with us sometimes."

As Tom charged onto the deck, Mrs. Wagner fell in step with him, trailing behind Punch and Skeeter down the steps to the dock. "Skeeter, I'll get in touch with your dad somehow. You and the boys should be here by six, please."

"Yes, ma'am," Skeeter said, very low.

"Will you see the dolphins today?" she went on. "I'm counting on going with you sometime. Your dad told us you have names for all of them."

"Yes, ma'am. Each one is different, acourse."

"And you recognize all of them?"

"Oh, yes, ma'am. That's easy. They're just like humans. We got a funny old man wanders all over the place, and a nervous, fussy old lady" — here he grinned widely — "and a coupla very sexy females that all the boys have their eyes on. A buncha young'uns, too, and three beautiful babies."

42

His voice turned serious. "But we got one that's worryin' everbody. Big Daddy. Somethin's wrong with his left flipper. It's awful pitiful."

Mmhmm, Punch thought, Why can't he be like this all the time? And then it hit him. *Dolphin* was the magic word.

Punch listened as Skeeter rattled off several facts about dolphins and thought, He'd fit right in with my class. Smart as anything.

"Come on," Punch said. "We've got lots of island to explore. 'Bye, Mom, see you later."

"Let's go, Skeeter," Tom said.

Skeeter went only as far as the middle of Taylor's Creek before he cut the engine. "Okay, what's goin' on?" he asked.

I am incredibly cool, Punch told himself. He stood up in the bow, deliberately casual, and fished in his pocket for toast, which he tossed into the air for the gulls.

"Skeeter," he began, "you don't want to do carpenter work. You hate it. You said so yourself."

Skeeter's eyes narrowed to icy slits. "I'd ruther earn money than get insulted."

Tom leapt in. "Punch wouldn't do that. He might slug you, but he doesn't say mean stuff. No way."

"You didn't understand me, Skeeter," continued Punch, "so you jumped to a dumb conclusion!" It was very satisfying to be able to accuse someone else of being impulsive.

"My family bein' all pitiful and poor, you mean?"

"See? Dumb conclusion! All I said was, you had a real good reason to hunt for treasure."

Skeeter leaned forward. "Let's get this straight. I don't need money. Me and Daddy are doin' fine. Carpenters don't make a whole lot — probly nothin' like college professors — but Daddy's the best in all Carteret County."

"That isn't it! It isn't even close!" yelled Punch. "Remember when I asked you if you were going to work at the marine lab? Remember that? Well, *that's* why you need this treasure. It's a real good reason and you haven't even thought about it!"

"The marine lab?" Skeeter repeated blankly. Then he gripped the sides of the skiff as if to steady himself. "I got it," he breathed. "I got it. Boy, am I thickheaded." He trembled all over as the idea took hold.

"I can be a dolphin professor!" he exulted, thinking aloud. "That's it, isn't it? That's what you meant?"

He rushed on without waiting for a reply. "I just never let myself thenk on it. It was a dream, see? Nobody in my family's ever been to college. But if we find the treasure, and if I help dig — that's only fair, I know — then I'll have plenty . . ." He stopped, breathless, gazing into the years ahead.

Punch felt the warmth of satisfaction. For sure, this was the real Skeeter Grace.

"You guys are *maximum strange*," said Tom, look-

44

ing from one to the other. "I *never* think about college. It's too far away and it's going to be a lot of work."

"You have to think about it at my house," Punch said. "We talk about it all the time." He looked at Skeeter. "And professors make hardly any money. This's our first real vacation, because now Mom's got a job at the art museum. Anyhow, college'll be okay, I guess. Lila can't wait."

Skeeter sighed. "She's the prettiest girl I ever saw. She's not stuck on herself, neither."

"She's way too old for you," Tom said firmly.

Punch gestured at the outboard. "Can we go now?"

"You bet!" cried Skeeter.

Under a fiery sun they began again to search for Blackbeard's treasure. This time all three of them dug, taking turns with the two spades, and this time they wore bathing suits and insect repellent and made frequent trips into the water.

Skeeter hopped in and out of the growing hole, testing here and there with the metal detector, swearing freely when no encouraging *beep, beep* sounded. "Goddam bugs," he said, swatting his shoulder. "Skeeters are bad this year."

Tom said, "That's your name. How'd you get it?"

"From Daddy. He said I was a little bitty theng as a kid. I ran everwhar, never walked. A flitty little

45

skeeter, see? Besides, my name's Rutherford. Who'd want a name like that?"

Tom leaned on his spade. "I wish I had a nickname."

"Nice guy in my class named Tom," Skeeter said. "Real good guy." He nodded at Punch. "How'd you get yours?"

"In gym. Second grade." The memory was clear. "Our school had a new punching bag and I went at it first. Bam, bam, bam, pretty fast. Pretending I was a real boxer. The gym teacher said, 'Hey, Punch, let somebody else have a turn,' and it stuck."

Skeeter gave him a fleeting smile and went back to digging. When they decided the hole was big enough, he tested it, evoking not a sound from the detector. Doggedly, they put back all the sand and started over.

By noon they lay exhausted in the shallows, cursing the long-dead pirate.

"Trouble is, he was crazy as a loon," Skeeter said.

"Who says he didn't sink it in the ocean?" asked Tom.

"He wasn't that big a fool. Tides change, currents shift. A few chests wouldn't stay put. Nah, it's buried somewhar on land."

They spent the rest of the day digging. They unearthed strange worms, unknown plants, ancient bottles, and bits of corroded metal. They came across fox dens, raccoon tracks, countless sea shells, and everywhere, horse droppings from the wild herd.

As Skeeter stepped out of the last hole he said,

"Nope. Let's get on home, Punch, before your momma has a hissy. Tomorra we'll make a list a good places at the library."

Tom heaved his shovel into the skiff. "Are we dead sure this treasure's still around?"

Skeeter's head bobbed up and down as he started the motor. "No lie. Tons and tons of it." He turned to Punch. "And we'll just keep huntin' till we find it, won't we?"

"Well, uh . . . sure," said Punch, who, while willing to hunt forever, was now less sure about finding something. And now it was important to find the treasure. Before, it had been a game, something fun to do on vacation.

How did this all happen? he wondered as Skeeter maneuvered across the busy waterway. It seemed like a terrific idea at first . . . I mean, I jumped on it! Uh-oh. Once again he had rushed headlong into something.

And here they were, with Skeeter all set to find pirate treasure — counting on it to make a dream come true. Hoo-ee, I've really done it this time. Punch's face was sober as he reached out to grab the post at the end of their dock.

At nine-thirty on Wednesday morning, Punch, Tom, and Skeeter settled in the library's reference section. Skeeter began reading the history of local islands, while

47

Tom selected a book on pirates. Punch chose a biography of Blackbeard.

He stared at a portrait of the pirate, an enormous hulk strong enough to throw a man overboard with one hand. His powerful arms resembled those of an ape, but it was the massive, thick beard that dominated the picture.

Punch read how Blackbeard twisted the ends of his beard into pigtails, tying them together and looping them over his ears. He took hemp cords and dipped them in saltpeter, sticking the cords among his pigtails and under his tricornered hat. Before a fight, he lit the cords to make them sputter and crackle like snakes on fire.

Wearing a blood-red sash stuffed with pistols and daggers, he roared into battle, screaming oaths. People often fainted at the sight of him.

Moreover, he was a clever captain, commandeering sloops until he had an entire fleet. Just before a fight at sea, he flew the flag with skull and crossbones.

Once when his men were sick, he blockaded the port of Charleston, holding people for ransom until he got chests of medicine. But mainly he was an evil person whose men were deathly afraid of him.

He even shot his most loyal man in the knee, crippling him for life. When asked why, he said, "Damn you for rogues! If I did not now and then kill one of you, you would forget who I am!"

Punch muttered, "He must have been totally wacko."

"I told you," Skeeter said, looking up. "But don't get all riled up. We got six years. I don't have to have it till then. Can y'all come back next summer?"

"Me? A terrible tourist?"

Skeeter giggled. "It's okay. You can't help it. But we get awful tired a tourists here, 'specially Yankees. You're both," he concluded.

That's me, the New Jersey Leper, Punch thought, remembering a recent Sunday school lesson. The ancient lepers had been forced to warn others of their approach by ringing a bell and crying, "Unclean!" Of course, leprosy was contagious and being a Yankee or a tourist wasn't.

"I think we are coming back," Punch said. "You can ask Dad, but don't tell him what we're doing. This's a secret."

"Right. We don't want everbody and their brother lookin'." Skeeter put his nose back in his book.

Tom said, "Hammock House was major, you know. All kinds of pirates hung out there. Guys like Stede Bonnet. He's a riot. He kept getting lost at sea! Couldn't navigate at all, it says. That's why he took up with Blackbeard."

Skeeter put his book down. "Shackleford Banks is major, too. Can't forget that. And Ocracoke Inlet. Blackbeard had a house up there. Big, fancy place."

"I'll start our list," Tom volunteered, heading for the front desk and a piece of paper.

They went back to reading. Punch learned about Blackbeard's wedding to Prudy Lutrelle, the sixteen-year-old from North Carolina. Only days after the marriage, he put Prudy — in chains — aboard his sloop and locked her in his cabin. No one saw her again.

It wasn't long before Blackbeard made his men row a heavy chest ashore and bury it on a tiny island. He swore the men to eternal silence, but one speculated in a journal that they hadn't buried treasure.

Most likely poor Prudy, Punch decided.

By noontime the boys had a list of several likely places. As they left the library Skeeter said, "Shackleford Banks is next, right?"

"Yeah, and it's going to take time," said Punch. "It'd be perfect if we could camp there, but I bet my folks say no." In frustration, he jammed his hands into his pockets. In the left pocket was toast for the gulls. In his right pocket was something small and hard.

Oh, yes. The skull from Blackbeard's yard.

5•
Yo, Ho, Ho, and a Bottle of Catsup

As the Wagners finished dinner Wednesday evening, Lanky and Skeeter Grace arrived. "We're here on a diplomatic mission," Mr. Grace said over pie and coffee.

"Sig, you remember those trips to Shackleford Banks? All that soulful music we made in the moonlight on those harmonicas my momma gave us?"

Both men laughed. Punch's dad said, "I caught my biggest fish off the Banks, too. Smoked my first and last cigarettes there" — he shook his head at Lanky, who still smoked — "and remember the year we had Hoopy Waller with us and we hid all his clothes?"

They chuckled again. Skeeter made a discreet thumbs-up sign at Punch and Tom.

"Well," Lanky continued, "I figure it's our boys' turn. I'll loan 'em our tents and the Coleman stove. We can run 'em out first theng tomorra."

Punch was impressed. How could anybody say no after a work-up like that?

"No, thank you," said his mother. "Shackleford is uninhabited. They'd be out there all alone."

Lanky's clear, aqua eyes crinkled at the corners. "That's the idea," he said. "Folks pay a lotta money to send kids to wilderness camps. We got one here, and it's free."

"They've already been gone three days! I wanted us to do things together." She looked from one male face to another. "Now I feel like a big wet blanket."

When no one answered, she began to walk up and down the kitchen. "Sig, I wish you'd think about this! What if something happened? How would we ever explain it to Tom's parents? It might be different if the boys were older."

Professor Wagner rubbed his little bald spot and looked unhappily at Punch.

She's winning, Punch thought. Up till now that had always been okay because she'd been persuading his dad to buy him cleats or shoulder pads, something his father didn't understand. But now, she was the one who didn't understand.

"I'll go, Mom." Everyone's head jerked in surprise as Lila spoke. Punch was dumbfounded as she continued.

"I've never been camping and kids keep saying how much fun it is, so I'll try it out with these guys. They won't care if I can't cook or set up a tent or make a fire."

Tom whispered to Punch. "We don't know about

that stuff either, and it's major when you're camping." For the first time he was regarding Lila with less than adoration.

Still, Punch beamed at his sister. She had rescued him in the past, but never so splendidly as now.

More discussion followed, but the outcome was no longer in doubt. They were going camping with Lila, who knew absolutely nothing about camping.

That evening Professor Wagner worked with Punch to gather supplies. He and his dad had rarely collaborated on a project. "First, sit calmly and make a list," said his father. "Then you'll have what you need."

Piles grew out on the deck and down on the dock. Punch thought they might as well move permanently to the island. He left the little skull behind, though. Just touching it made him uneasy. I should throw it away, he thought angrily, but somehow he couldn't, and so he shoved it into the far corner of his dresser drawer.

At eight Thursday morning, Lanky and Skeeter helped to load everything into Skeeter's boat and the Wagners' rented skiff. Then they cruised out past Carrot Island to Shackleford Banks, almost a mile and a half from Beaufort. Punch's dad began to set up tents, and Mr. Grace left for work. As he anchored Lila's tent, Professor Wagner said, "I can take your place if you've changed your mind. I haven't camped in years, but I remember how."

"No thanks, Dad." Lila was wearing a black shirt knotted at the waist, cutoff jeans, and a red bandanna tied around her head. "We're going to play pirate and you don't know how." She patted his head. "Better get out of the sun or put on a cap. Your bald spot's burning."

When the tents were in place, Professor Wagner said, "Okay, you're set. This is a good, big flag and I want you to keep it raised. Mom and I'll be able to see it from our deck through the binoculars. If you pull it down, we'll come right away.

"Remember that Shackleford is a wilderness area, so be careful campers. Lanky can bring anything you need from town when he comes each night. You guys mind Lila and keep putting on suntan lotion." He paused, looking thoughtful, and then a smile took over. "I guess that's enough of a farewell speech. Have fun, okay?"

As soon as his dad had started the outboard, Punch turned to his sister, "What do you mean 'play pirate'?"

"I'm not blind. I heard you tell Dad those spades were for digging bathroom holes, but that's not all they're for, I bet. You're still looking for treasure, aren't you?"

Punch nodded.

"Okay," she went on, "so you have to think like pirates. Do what they did. The whole bit. Maybe that's

54

why nobody's found it so far. They didn't really *get into it*."

The boys looked at her with amazement. "Do you want to hunt, too?" Punch asked.

"No. I came here to get away from Johnny Keith." She made a face and Punch nodded, understanding.

Tom's hands turned into fists and his face reddened. "If that turkey —" he began.

"Don't worry," Lila hastily assured him. "I just decided to take a break before he got too carried away." She adjusted her bandanna to a jauntier angle.

"Now," she said, "let's say I'm one of those famous girl pirates . . . only I don't dig. You guys can do that." She grinned. "I don't need much treasure anyway. Just enough for the Juilliard School. I'm not greedy."

"Hah!" said Punch. "Dad said that place costs a fortune!"

"Blackbeard hid a fortune. All you have to do is find it. Now let's get lunch and you guys can take a nap."

"Nap?" chorused three voices.

"Look up there!" She pointed at the sun. "Do you really think pirates dug big holes in this heat? Of course not. They worked at night when it was cooler and nobody could see them. You guys need to get into this right now!"

We'd better humor her, Punch decided, so we can stay out here. "Uh, right," he said. "Avast, me hearties! I starveth, forsooth!"

Tom hooted.

Lila said, "That's the idea."

"Yankees are purely crazy." Skeeter shook his head.

Rummaging in the boxes of food, Lila said, "Did we bring any hardtack or salt pork or beef jerky? Any cans of greasy stew or biscuit mix for dumplings?"

"Why would we do that?" cried Punch.

"Because it'd be so nice and authentic," she explained. "Sailors and pirates — anybody who lived on those old ships — had horrible food. No fresh fruit, and everybody got scurvy, remember? So we can't eat any fresh fruit. I hope we have lots of coffee. They lived on coffee."

Punch looked at Skeeter. "Yup, crazy," he said.

Lila finished checking groceries. "Well, it's too bad, but all we've got is normal stuff," she said. "I guess you can make a fire and do hot dogs."

"Yo ho ho, and a bottle of catsup!" Tom shouted happily. "Avast, men! Mayhap we should hunteth for driftwood."

"Perfect," said Lila, giving him her most glowing smile.

Mayhap I puketh, thought Punch as he helped Tom and a giggling Skeeter pick up driftwood.

The pirates felt better after lunch, but not cooler. They stretched out in the shade to wait for evening.

"Dream about being pirates," Lila told them. "I'm going to read and later we'll go swimming."

Perhaps because he was hot and slept poorly, or

perhaps because she had suggested it, Punch did dream. He was a dolphin, frolicking in the water, playing hide-and-seek with other dolphins. He squeaked to tell them when to hide, and then he hunted them down, gliding swiftly through the water, feeling it whoosh past his streamlined head and body. He found the others easily by emitting sound waves that bounced off their bodies and echoed back to him.

When the oldest male told everyone to swim east toward the tall human's house, the dolphin Punch grew uneasy. He had heard that the tall human was evil and so he tried to tell the others. No one listened. He thrust himself ahead of them and stood up on his tail to cry repeated warnings. Still they streamed eastward until they were offshore from a white house on a hummock of ground.

At the old one's command they rose up on their tails, looking toward the hummock. The dolphin Punch could see what was happening there. Many men had gathered around a woman with beautiful red-gold hair. She was screaming and sobbing — fearful sounds that pierced the air.

It was Lila. She had been captured by Blackbeard, whose laughter roared across the water as she screamed and struggled. "Punch!" she cried. "Punch!"

"Lila!" he shrieked. Only it came out as a squeak and a whistle, because he was a dolphin and he could not help her.

"Punch! Hey, Punch, wake up!"

"Lila —" he gasped, coming to awareness. He sat up, drenched in sweat and breathing fast.

Lila was kneeling beside him. He grabbed her arm and said, "Whoa," in a quivery voice. "Wait'll you hear *this*."

"Tell me in the water. I'm burning up." And later, when he had told her, she said, "Wow. The mind is so weird. I've always planned on majoring in music, but the more I think about psychology, the more I like it. Do you think Dad would just croak?"

Before he could answer, Tom and Skeeter joined them in the water and the talk shifted to fishing. Mr. Grace would be arriving soon with bait so they could catch their supper. Lila approved. "I bet pirates ate a lot of fish," she said.

At sundown, after his dad had come and gone, Skeeter rigged poles and arranged his men at the water's edge.

"Daddy didn't have much bait for us, so y'all better catch somethin', even if it's just more fish for bait."

He showed how to cast near the edge of a sandbar they'd found while swimming. "Maybe we'll luck inta some red drum. This's the best time to fish for 'em and they're good."

Minutes went by and no one caught anything. "Just keep castin'," Skeeter urged.

Darkness had dimmed the water's surface when Tom yelled, "Hey, help!"

Skeeter hastily wedged the handle of his pole in

drier sand behind him and ran to where Tom stood, feet sinking rapidly.

"You got one, you got one!" Skeeter hopped up and down in the water. "Reel him in slow — slow, now."

Tom kept sinking as he pulled back on his pole, reeling in a few more feet, then a few more, until he had to squat down, using his rear end as an anchor against the swirling surf and the pull of the fish.

"He's big," Tom panted, "real big. Look at the bend in my pole! Geez!"

When the fish was at last in the shallows, struggling in the dip net, Skeeter said, "Purely amazin', Tom! This's a six, seven-pound drum! Wait'll we tell Daddy."

Skeeter barbecued the fish as steaks over a wood fire. He tucked other steaks into one of the ice-filled coolers.

"Best fish I ever ate," Lila said. "Let's have the rest for breakfast."

By now the moon had risen above the low, wind-swept trees. Punch and Skeeter got their spades and nudged the lump on the sand. "Heave ho, me hearty," said Punch.

Tom groaned. "I ateth a ton. Leave me here, okay?"

"Forty lashes," Lila said, laughing.

Very soon she was waving them off. "Have fun, you guys. I'll be right here. Don't do anything dumb."

The boys aimed for the highest dunes on the island. At the top, they stopped to survey the area while the moon rose above them.

"See thar?" said Skeeter, pointing across the water. "That's Lenoxville Point, on the edge a Beaufort. I been thinkin', and if I was Blackbeard, I coulda stood on that point and sighted right out here to this dune."

"Hey, that's brilliant," Punch said.

"Acourse. And one time Papaw said this high place had been here forever. So it's a real good place."

Punch thought about New Jersey sand dunes and how they were formed. He didn't want to dig any more than necessary. "Down there," he said, "at the base. Not here on top. I bet these dunes just get taller and taller on the windy side."

Skeeter shot him a quick look. "Not bad for a tourist."

"You must think we're all dodos!"

"Nossir. We had a real smart one coupla seasons ago."

Punch looked at him and sure enough, Skeeter was holding back laughter.

"Ya hah hah," Punch said with heavy sarcasm.

They got busy digging, working toward a hole about two feet deep and six feet in diameter. When they finished, Skeeter passed the metal detector all across the bottom. *Beep, beep, beep, beep,* it sang.

"Keep it there!" hollered Punch, leaping into the hole. Sand spewed out behind him as he dug.

Clink, sounded the spade. Punch stopped. He probed gently. *Clink.*

"I thenk I'm gonna pass out," Skeeter said, hands clenched around the metal detector.

Punch dug to one side of the clink and Tom on the other. With careful scooping, they revealed a rectangular top of something. Something small. Certainly not a wooden chest with iron bands.

Punch inched the spade down on all sides until he was able to wedge it underneath and bring up the object. He dusted off the sandy dirt.

"Just a metal box," he said.

They pushed up on the lid, but it wouldn't budge, so Tom pulled out his Swiss army knife and went to work, forcing the top to give way finally with a metallic squeak.

All three grasped the box and peered inside.

The biggest thing was a Bible, its leather cover intact. Next to it were strands of cream-colored beads tangled up with several women's brooches, two tiny, black spoons, and a dark metal chain.

Skeeter let go of the box. "Museum'll wanta see this," he said heavily. He walked away and sat down, hunched over.

"Hey, come on," Punch said, moved by the small, abject figure. "Somebody thought this was a great place to bury stuff! I'll bet it's real old, too." He flipped open the Bible, turning pages until he came to a list of names.

"Samuel Z. White," he read, angling the Bible so

that the moon shone on the page. "Born 1659, Died 1720."

He looked up from the spidery writing. "You hear that, Skeeter? He could have been here when Blackbeard stayed at Hammock House. It's perfect!"

Tom held up the strands of beads. "I bet this old jewelry's worth something. Lila will know. We can dig more later. Come on, Skeeter."

6•
Heave Ho, Me Hearties

Lila looked up from the contents of the box. "I think you guys really found something." In her "mother" voice she added, "Aren't you proud of yourselves?"

"We'd be a lot prouder if it were a real treasure chest," Punch said. He leaned back against her tent and looked up at the perfect night — stars winking down on them, moon bright on the white sand. Like Carrot Island, Shackleford was another piece of heaven on earth. He wanted it to have buried treasure, too.

Tom said, "I bet this stuff's worth real money."

Skeeter moved closer. "I don't need the Bible. Mamaw gave me one for Sunday school when I was little."

Lila looked at him for a long moment, then bent her head over the things in the box. "The jewelry and the baby spoons should be worth something, and if the chain's gold, we're talking megabucks."

"See there," Tom said, looking smug. "We're on our way. Slap me five!" He held his hand out to Skeeter.

Lila tipped her head to one side. "Okay, this is the head pirate speaking. Why're you guys so serious?"

Punch knew better than to try to fool her. "Well, see, when I first got this idea —"

"Let me do it," Skeeter said, proceeding with much gesturing and no pauses until at last he said, "Lila, nobody ever figured this out before — that I should be a dolphin professor — but right off, first night I met him, Punch says, 'Are you gonna do that when you grow up?' Isn't that purely amazin'?"

He stopped to breathe and Lila jumped in. "So you think Blackbeard's treasure will pay your way through college?"

"Acourse!"

"Wow." She looked from one boy to the other. "It'll be tough, you know. You're going to have to keep the faith."

At her words, Punch's spirit lifted and again took wings. She was right, and his idea was *not* impossible. Already they'd found something that had been buried for over two hundred years. They just had to keep on believing.

"Heave ho, me hearties!" he boomed.

"First, matey, a drink," Tom said. "Digging maketh me very thirsty."

When they set out again they carried a bottle of Gatorade and a box of graham crackers. Lila stood by her tent, draped in her sheet against the damp ocean air, and called, "Good luck!" as they went away from her.

Punch turned to wave, but her appearance stopped him. In the moonlight her hair had become a fiery cloud, and her sheet, the raiments of a ghost, shimmering eerily in the breeze.

His skin prickled. This was how he had felt in that weird dream, and before that, in the uncanny chill of Blackbeard's yard when he had held the skull.

Blackbeard's yard. The next place on their list — in spite of Skeeter's fear.

I'm not going to think about that, he told himself. We're here now and we've got good places to dig. He ran to catch up with Tom and Skeeter.

Back at the foot of the dunes, they hastily filled in the hole that had yielded their first treasure and began a new excavation.

"Suppose we don't find the big treasure," Tom said after a time. "If we found enough jewelry boxes, we'd do great!"

"Sure," Punch said. "Or we could find some other pirate's treasure. That'd be okay."

Skeeter leaned thoughtfully on his spade. "We *could* find more boxes," he said. "There was a whole town out here. Everbody was inta whalin' on the Banks back then. Their houses are all gone now. Burned down, I heard."

"Dig, motor-mouth," Punch said.

"Why would they bury stuff?" asked Tom.

"Storms," Skeeter replied. "Big storm comes and your whole place just blows away." He gazed seaward. "See, that box we found coulda belonged to somebody whose house just disappeared in one a those famous hurricanes. Took 'em right along with it, I reckon, and they never got back here —"

"Dig!" cried Tom, panting with effort.

"Relax," Skeeter said. "Y'all are just like ever Yankee born. Got no more patience than a gnat."

Clink, sounded Tom's shovel. *Clink, clink*.

Punch grabbed the metal detector and leapt into the hole. *Beep, beep* went the detector in one place. *Beep, beep* in another.

"Hotdamn!" yelled Skeeter.

The new treasure was soon out on the sand. Eight beer cans, ten soft-drink cans, metal pop-tops, and wads of aluminum foil lay beside a torn plastic sack.

"A garbage dump. Big whup," Punch said, heaving it back into one corner of the hole. "They sure didn't bury it very far. Our garbage hole at camp is lots deeper."

Several huge excavations later, the Gatorade and graham crackers were history. Punch had four old square nails in his pocket, which they would take to the museum. Skeeter had a few odd bits that might have once been fishhooks. Tom had three cream-colored buttons. They all had aching backs.

Wearily they slogged home through the sand to camp.

Late the next morning Skeeter cooked the rest of the drum and Tom and Punch toasted bread over one side of the fire. It was nearly noon when they scrubbed their plates with sand and water, and again it was muggy and hot. Punch fed their breakfast remains to the gulls, making sure that the little one with the damaged claw got the most.

When Skeeter found that Lila's tent was the breeziest place in camp, the three boys crept inside and stretched out.

"Last night must have been really hard work," Lila said when she saw them. "You old sea dogs better sleep, I guess. See you in a few hours."

When they woke, she took them to a tiny cove she had found on the seaward side of the island. "What do you think, men?"

Punch tried thinking as a pirate captain. "Yo ho, bilge and barnacles," he mumbled, "I'm sailing on the bounding main, looking for a place to hide all these chests of jewels and silver, and I see this weeny little bay. . . ." He glanced around the cove. "Yup," he said. "I like it. Men, what do you think?"

"It's not so danged big. We could really check it out," Skeeter observed. "But we're huntin' in a good place now. We have to finish thar first."

As he spoke, a pair of loons flew into the cove and settled on the water, all the time making their strange, haunting call.

"Don't usually see 'em this time a year," Skeeter said. "They're real good eatin'. I'd ruther have a loon than a turkey anyday."

Lila put her hands on her hips. "Our book says it

isn't legal to shoot them anymore. You don't do that, do you?"

"We always have," Skeeter replied.

Lila managed to appear older, taller, and morally outraged all at once. "That's the dumbest reason I ever heard! Some people hunt dolphins, too. They always have."

Skeeter looked stricken. "That's terrible! Who'd wanta hurt a dolphin?"

"Yeah!" chimed Punch. And then, curiously, he thought of the fish, the beautiful red drum they had caught and then eaten. What made some species sacred and not others?

Tom slapped him on the rear. "Come on, Punch baby, we're going swimming."

Around six, Lanky Grace arrived, told Lila she was getting sunburned, and left behind two full crab pots plus a bag of spices called "crab boil." As he left he called back, "Same time tomorra evenin'! Y'all mind Lila, hear?"

"Uh-oh," Skeeter said as his dad's boat roared away. "We need a great big pot."

"Got one," Punch said. He had argued for some time with his father over this pot, insisting they would never need it unless someone wanted to take a bath, which was insane.

His father had said, "Always take a big pot on a

camping trip. It's one of those small but important things."

Now, Skeeter put water in the pot and rigged a holding net inside it for the wiggling crabs, just above the steaming water. "You sprinkle 'em with some of that crab boil, Punch, before I pop this lid on. These are so goo-ood . . . make you slap your granmammy."

Twenty-four delicious crabs later, Lila and the pirates sat over mugs of coffee. The boys had never had coffee before, but Lila felt strongly about doing things right.

"Okay," Punch said, sipping the bitter brew and wondering why anyone liked it. "We better get at it."

That Friday night stretched into the longest and hardest night in his memory. They dug and filled and dug and filled again. As dawn approached, regular mounds at the base of the dunes testified to their thoroughness.

"We've only got one more night," Skeeter mourned.

"Better go to Lila's cove then," said Punch.

Saturday drifted by in a series of naps and small meals. No one really came alive until suppertime, except for Lila, who read and continued to explore the island.

That evening Lila opened a can of Spam and said to pretend it was salt pork. The bread represented greasy dumplings, and the carrot sticks were beef jerky. She poured thick, black coffee into their mugs. "Camp cooking is fun," she said. "I didn't think I'd like it."

"I don't," Punch said, regarding his coffee.

After supper the boys lolled in the water, waiting for Mr. Grace. "Lots of folks camp out here to watch for ghost ships," Skeeter told them. "They see 'em, too, 'specially durin' hurricane season. Bad weather, ship can go down with all hands. Most ever family we know lost folks like that."

Punch pointed to an approaching skiff. "I think this's your dad," he said. "We'll tell him we explored the west end of the island today, how's that?"

As Skeeter's father was leaving he asked, "Y'all gettin' bored? I can carry y'all home if you want. We can come back for the big stuff in the mornin'."

"No, Daddy, we're havin' fun," Skeeter insisted. "Tomorra noon's soon enough."

Within minutes of his departure, they set out for the tiny cove across the island. The moon shone brilliantly down upon them as they dug their first hole.

"I hope we find something," Tom said as he dumped a huge spadeful. "Last night was a bummer."

"Yup, sure was, but it's *got to be here somewhere*," replied Punch, stoking the fire of their faith.

"Yeah," Skeeter agreed, "except y'all put Hammock House next and that's purely crazy."

Punch and Tom quit digging and looked at each other. Nobody wants to think about it, Punch decided as he watched Tom's face. *And I just know it's the most logical place.*

"It's dumb to worry about stuff ahead of time," he said, deliberately offhand. He threw himself back into digging with increased fervor.

Thunk went his spade. *Thunk* again.

"Finally!" Tom cried, hopping over to help him dig. Skeeter leapt into the hole and used his hands to scoop away loose sand. They unearthed a wooden crate, its sides jagged and splintery. Several dark bottles lay nearby, perhaps the contents of the broken crate.

To the right of the bottles was another box, intact, but badly weathered. "Washed up in a storm, betcha anytheng," Skeeter whispered excitedly. "We could find all kinds a stuff here!"

Just below the second box lay the remains of a suitcase, which disintegrated in feathery particles as they lifted it from its grave. Old-fashioned men's clothing had been packed inside — two gray vests, funny-looking underwear, wool socks, and a yellowed shirt with pearly buttons down its pleated front. Stained with seawater, the garments were still whole.

The last object was a tightly packed, leather carryall. "Books," Punch said, sighing as he undid the flap and dumped them out. "Why couldn't it have been a big jewelry box?"

"Not all books," Tom said, grinning broadly. He held up a rectangular container. "This was inside that thick one and it isn't a book. Yo ho HO, said the big bad pirate!"

Each boy took one of the square glass decanters and forced the darkened metal caps to unscrew. Eyeing his, Tom said, "Vodka, I bet. My grampa drinks it."

Punch said, "Go ahead, try it."

Tom looked uncertain. "Maybe it isn't good anymore."

"Some big bad pirate you are!" taunted Skeeter.

"Okay, okay!" Tom closed his eyes and took a swallow.

Skeeter, too, lifted his bottle and drank. He coughed violently and said, "Whee-euw! I thenk it's whiskey."

Tom let out a long, rasping breath. "Wow!" he said.

Punch tipped up his bottle. Okay, he thought, at least it'll be cool after being buried so deep. They had used the last ice from their coolers that morning and he longed for a drink of something really cold.

He swallowed, choked, swallowed again, and gasped, "Man! I don't know what it is, but it's powerful!"

"It kind of grabs your throat," Tom said, "but it's cold and I'm thirsty." He took another long drink.

Skeeter examined the container that had held the three decanters of liquor. "Pretty sneaky. Looks just like a big book." He tipped his bottle up again. "I'm kinda gettin' used to mine. Tastes better than it did."

"Mine, too," Punch agreed, taking his third or fourth swallow. He knew he shouldn't. He and Tom had

72

heard many lectures in health class about the dangers of alcohol. Tonight, he scooted back against the dunes and put all that out of his mind.

"Sixteen men on a dead man's chest," he warbled. "I bet it was fun being a pirate. Sailing all day long . . . singing songs . . . robbing rich people . . . all kinds of parties like this. Yup —" Here he felt a bit strange and so he had another nice, cold drink.

"Oh, I'm a dirty pirate and I've gotta have my rum," he sang, voice wobbling off-key. Tom and Skeeter booed.

"No, wait — wait, you guys. I got one!" He began again. "Smarty Arty had a party. No one came but Tommy Farty." He pounded Tom on the back and chortled with appreciation at his own wit.

"Oh, yeah?" Tom pounded back and together they fell over on the sand, wrestling. Tom pulled himself up and frowned down at Punch. "Tell me what you had for lunchy. Pukey food and poopy Punchy."

"Heh, heh, heh, poopy Punchy," tittered Skeeter. "And it could be pukey Punchy. Or pukey poopy Punchy." He held out his decanter. "Y'all trade bottles with me. Mine's gettin' borin'."

Everyone tried a different liquor. Punch yawned and then yawned again. This was great fun, but so tiring. His head felt awfully heavy. "Here, Skeeter-Peter," he said, handing back his decanter.

Skeeter frowned. "Yankee tourist."

Punch tried to hold his head still in order to glare

at Skeeter. "What does that have to do with anything?" he asked, his good mood shattered.

Skeeter's mouth fell open in a silly grin. "Nothin', but it sure yanks your chain. Heh, heh, heh."

"Hey, guys," Tom began, a bewildered look on his face.

"Don't 'hey' *me!*" snapped Skeeter. "It's a free country. I can say what I want. And this whole theng is purely crazy. A buncha kids can't find buried treasure. And it's our treasure, anyhow. You got no right to come down here and carry it off!"

Punch's jaw jutted forward. "Finders keepers!" he growled. "If I find it, I'm keeping it!"

"Y'are not! I'm goin' to college with it!"

Tom lumbered in between them. "Shut up!" he said. With his left hand he pushed Punch down into the sand on his left. He did the same to Skeeter on his right.

"Just cool it," Tom said thickly. "See the moon up there? That means bedtime. Big sleepy time."

"Okay, okay," Punch said, closing his eyes. It felt wonderful to lie absolutely still on the cool sand in the moonlight.

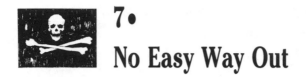

7•
No Easy Way Out

He was swimming through a vast ocean, swimming hard. He thrashed his arms and kicked wildly, tossing his head from side to side as he battled the endless sea. Miles of salty water . . . and he was so thirsty. He licked his lips and thought, No, no, don't swallow it, it'll make you sick.

"Punch! Please, Punch, wake up, *please!*"

Wake up? The words registered slowly. It was a dream, then, and he wasn't really swimming in the ocean. He was good at scaring himself in dreams.

Punch stopped thrashing and lay still. This time, though, the dream stayed with him even as he came awake. The seawater and the thirst were real. So, too, the sick feeling in his stomach.

"Come on, Punch. What's going on here, anyway? I've been scared to death."

"Lila?" he asked weakly, squinting up at her. His insides churned and bubbled, promising to erupt.

"Wow, were you out! You still are. Want me to pour more water on you?"

76

Ah. That explained all the water.

"No, no," he groaned as he forced himself to sit up. That's when his head split into two parts. He felt around for it on the sand, so that he could put it back together and set it on his neck where it belonged, but he couldn't find it.

Lila knelt in front of him and put one cool hand on either side of his face. Oh, that felt good. His head must not have cracked in half after all; it was there under her hands where it ought to be.

"Punch, I smelled those bottles. Did you guys drink that liquor? And where'd it come from?"

Liquor. He remembered now. His stomach lurched and his parched mouth filled with saliva and the taste of bile.

"Oh, look out, I'm going to —" He never made it to his feet. Bent double, he vomited between his legs, retching over and over until his stomach muscles burned with pain and tears spurted from his eyes.

When he finished spitting out the last of it, he wiped one hand across his mouth and stared down at his humiliation, a revolting slime all over him and the sand. He closed his eyes and began to cry.

"Oh, brother," Lila said softly. "Come on. You can wash off in the water." She pulled him erect with both hands and they went together into the surf.

Punch couldn't look at her. He just wanted to crawl off somewhere and die alone.

Lila splashed him vigorously, reminding him of

times past when they'd had water fights. He had no fight in him now.

"Get busy and help and stop feeling sorry for yourself."

He rinsed himself then, until, after a long time, he felt clean. His head throbbed with every movement, but his stomach had subsided.

Watching him Lila said, "I guess I don't have to ask whether you drank that stuff or not."

Punch hung his head.

"Geez, and I thought you were bright." She shook her head in the way of all motherly souls. "You'd better help me with the other guys and just pray they didn't kill themselves." Frowning in concern she bent over Tom, spreadeagled in the sun like a kayoed boxer.

Later, after Tom and Skeeter had been helped to wake up, throw up, and clean up, Lila pointed to a clump of scrub trees and said, "Sit there where it's cooler."

They sat.

"Quit staring at your feet, you guys. Do you know how scared I've been? When you didn't come back to camp and didn't come back? If one of you had croaked, it would've been my fault! I'm in charge out here!" Her voice rose.

"I didn't need to do this, you know! I did it so you could hunt for treasure. Hah! Some treasure!" One arm flared in the direction of the boxes they had found. "And you should see yourselves! Geez!"

Punch felt worse and worse, if such a thing were possible. He had never seen his sister like this. Never.

He made himself look at her. "We didn't drink that much — at least I don't think so — but it was nice and cold, and after a while we forgot how it tasted. I know it was dumb. It's the dumbest thing I ever did."

"Is this a hangover?" Tom asked in a pained voice.

Skeeter got shakily to his feet and hurried behind the bushes. Everyone sat rigid, listening to him vomit again. Just hearing him made Punch's stomach revolt anew.

Sometime later, when they thought they had finished throwing up, Lila said, "Okay. There's just one thing. I won't talk if you guys promise never to do anything like this again. I mean, you really could have died." Her eyes bored into each boy in turn.

No one argued with her.

"I'm waiting for your promise," she said, head high.

"I promise," three voices said together.

"Deal. So I won't tell. Now come on, there's a lot of work back at camp before the folks come to pick us up. And when they get here, we had a terrific time, got it? *Every minute on Shackleford Banks was wonderful.*"

"Yes, ma'am," whispered Skeeter. "Thank you, ma'am. Do you have any aspirin?"

"Back at camp," Lila said, beginning to sound more

79

normal. She gestured toward their excavation. "We should take that crate and the old clothes and books, but just bury the container and those liquor bottles in your hole."

Punch and Tom set to work in mournful silence.

Skeeter moaned, "I swear somebody took a ball-bat to my head, and my eyes are killin' me in this sun."

Punch and Tom kept on shoveling. This was going to be some day.

Long hours later, when they were home and had helped put away the camping gear, Tom announced to the family, "Well, that was a really awesome camp-out!" His hearty voice made Punch's head throb.

"Awesome," Tom repeated while Lila looked on and nodded. "But I'm used to more sleep, so I think I'll take a little nap. Is that okay with you, Mrs. Wagner?"

"Of course, Tom. I promised your folks we'd call later when you were here, but you'll be awake by then."

"Oh, sure. If I'm not, get me up. I can be a real sack-rat sometimes. Hah, hah, hah."

"Punch, do you want a nap, too?" asked his dad as Tom disappeared upstairs. "You guys look pretty strung out."

"Oh, maybe a teeny one," Punch said, edging toward the stairs. Mozart followed; he had stayed close since Punch's return. "We probably talked too late last night. Dumb, huh? But it was fun. Best trip of my life!"

Up in their room, Tom was already face-down on his bed. Mozart hopped onto Punch's bed, pawed the pillow into an acceptable state, and sank down with a canine sigh of content. This is more like it, he seemed to say. A dog shouldn't have to sleep alone.

"Move, Mozie." Punch placed himself with care on the bed. He felt as if he might break, especially his head. He thought, Smart money says stay in bed for the rest of vacation. Vacation? What a dopey thing to call this.

Punch and Tom didn't see Skeeter for the rest of the weekend. Perhaps his dad and grandparents felt as Mrs. Wagner so obviously did — eager for family time.

Saturday evening the family went out to dinner, which Punch and Tom ate with caution, mindful of their queasy stomachs. Both boys, aware of Lila's eyes upon them, continued to rave about their camping trip.

On Sunday they went to Atlantic Beach, where the boys lay unmoving on their towels. As they toured nearby Fort Macon later, Tom said to Punch, "I guess we're going to live, huh?"

Punch didn't even think about the unopened crate until they returned home late Sunday afternoon.

"I'll get a crowbar from the shed," said Professor Wagner when he saw the old nails in the crate.

"Be awfully careful, Sig," warned Mrs. Wagner. "The museum staff will strangle us if we damage the find in any way." Turning her attention to the old clothes, the leather tote, and the books, she asked, "How did you happen to find these things? I know the museum is going to be excited."

Punch and Tom exchanged glances and Tom moseyed to the refrigerator to get juice. I'm on, thought Punch, who hated having to lie to his parents.

"We were just digging around, something to do," he said. "We were in a little cove on the far side of the island, and we thought, hey, what if a ship got wrecked out there and stuff washed up?" A sidelong glance at Lila rewarded him with an approving, though barely detectable, smile.

His dad wormed the crowbar underneath the lid of the crate and pried up in several places. One nail began to give and another, until rusty nails showed all around and the lid clattered to the kitchen floor.

Please, Punch prayed, eyes closed, please let it be something great. We've worked so hard.

"Oh, lovely!" his mother said. "A real treasure."

His eyelids flew open and he leaned forward to peer in, bumping heads with Tom on the opposite side of the crate. They looked down at their find, then up at each other.

Nestled in packing material that might once have been sawdust lay several tins, their colors still bright. Darkened gilt writing and elegant designs extolled the quality of the cloves, nutmeg, ginger, and teas inside the containers.

Her face alight, Mrs. Wagner held up one of the tins. "Fine tea and spices from the tropics were worth a fortune long ago. People used to buy spices in tiny packets and use them only for festive occasions. The museum here should be thrilled with what you've found. I know ours would be."

"Yup," Punch said. "Real luck, huh, Tom?"

Tom pulled a strip of dead skin from the healing sunburn on his arm. "Real luck," he echoed. "You suppose we could get lucky with some fish? Maybe catch another drum?"

"Mmhmm," said Punch's mother. "It sounded delicious when you told us about it. Why don't you try now? I don't care if we eat late."

"Good idea," said Professor Wagner. "Mozart and I'll zip out to the bait shop and be back for you guys in a few minutes."

Very soon, with Mozart as a live, vocal figurehead, they were on their way to the far side of Carrot Island, where they let the boat drift over the shoals.

"Eelgrass," said Professor Wagner, pointing to the narrow fronds waving just under the water. "Lanky and I used to find all kinds of stuff in eelgrass beds — scallops, crabs, little fish, sea horses, you name it."

"Sea horses?" Punch asked.

"Scallops?" Tom lingered over the word. "I love scallops. We almost never get any because Mom says they cost too much. I'll look for them and you guys fish."

"Sorry," Punch's dad said. "They're out of season in August, but you could hunt for clams with your toes. I make a mean chowder if I've got fresh clams."

Tom quickly shed his shoes and vaulted out of the boat. When it quit rocking after his departure, Punch slipped overboard, saying he would hunt for sea horses.

Professor Wagner looked from one to the other. "But now I'm the only one fishing!"

"I'll be back," Punch said, examining the eelgrass beds. "I want to see if I can find a sea horse first." He flexed his fingers hopefully.

Tom's head disappeared and he came up with a clam in each hand. "Piece of cake," he chortled as he waded to the boat and tossed in the clams.

Punch's father joggled his fishing line. "I can taste that chowder now. Boy, this is fun. I'm not sure where the money's coming from, but we'll be back next year."

"I got one!" Punch bent over his cupped hands. "Look, Tom, quick."

"Hi, guy," Tom said, his nose only inches from the sea horse. He tickled its tail as the miniature armored horse drifted in the prison of Punch's hands. "Man, is he teeny! How'd you ever find him?"

"It's a family gift," said Professor Wagner as he leaned over the side of the boat. "Let me see him,

84

just for a second. Then you should let him go. Mozart! Get on the other side before we tip over!"

Punch made himself release the tiny horse of the seas and climbed back into the boat to help his dad fish for dinner. Evening turned into night as they cast repeatedly with no luck, and Mozart barked at the persistent gulls.

Tom, meanwhile, devoted himself to clams. By the time Punch and his dad gave up, he had found more than enough.

"I don't think Mom was expecting supper to be this late," said Punch as they drew up alongside their dock.

"When she knows I'm the cook she won't care," his father observed.

Much later, in bed for the night, Tom said, "This is the coolest vacation I ever had. No lie."

"Yeah. And it's fun having a roommate." Punch hoped that didn't sound mushy or dumb. He had often wished he had a brother.

"That'll be one good thing about college," Tom admitted.

College, Punch thought, his mind flying back to Skeeter and his problem. The weekend away from treasure hunting had been a relief. But now one entire week was gone — so fast.

"Tomorrow's Monday," he said.

"Yeah. Are we really going to hunt at Hammock House?"

Punch wiggled his feet against Mozart while he tried to think of a way out — someplace better than the spooky white house. He had tried to forget the feelings that overtook him in the pirate's yard and he couldn't do it. He couldn't forget the tiny skull, either.

"Punch?"

"We'll take Mozart," he said at last, his mind made up. There was no easy way out. Not this time. Somehow he had known all along that he would dig the ground in Blackbeard's yard.

8•
Time of Dread

On Monday, the beginning of their second week of vacation, Punch and Tom prepared to take their treasure to the North Carolina Maritime Museum in Beaufort. Mrs. Wagner insisted that they wear good shorts and shirts as well as their best sneakers.

Skeeter arrived early, attired in ugly brown shoes, a clean T-shirt, and threadbare jeans. His damp hair had resisted the comb and was still a hay-heap, only clean. But his enthusiasm was unbounded as he explained his plan for a triumphant arrival in the museum curator's office with each member of the family bearing a treasure.

Lila looked up from her cello and waved her bow in the air. "Not me," she said. "I got up early to practice. You guys found that stuff, anyway."

Punch's mom agreed. "It's your show, boys. But come right back and tell us what the curator said, okay?"

So it was only the three boys who putted up Taylor's Creek in the fresh, sun-gold morning, their discoveries shrouded in Mr. Grace's old dropcloth. In the prow, Mozart was on guard as usual, barking at the sassy gulls that wheeled and dipped just out of reach.

"After the museum, we go to the jeweler's with the good stuff, okay?" said Skeeter. "Daddy says it might take awhile for an appraisal. That's when an expert says what this stuff'll sell for. Boy, I can't wait! Might not be much — you never know — but it'll be a start, it'll be a start!"

Punch grinned. "Did you swallow a bubble machine?"

"Who me? Oh, you thenk I'm talkin' too much again." He rushed on, unself-conscious as a baby. "See, I'm all excited because now Daddy knows, and he wasn't mad or disappointed or angry, nothin' bad a-tall."

"Knows what?" asked Punch. "You didn't tell him!"

"Nah, not about the treasure. That's a secret! See, I was explainin' how we'd split the money we got from the jewelry, and the spoons, and that big gold chain — "

"Maybe gold," Tom interrupted. "We aren't sure."

"Well, I am! Why else would they hide it so good? Anyway, I was tellin' him how we were diggin', just in case a shipwreck or somethin' like that, and there was this metal box fulla valuable stuff, and we were sharin' the money so I could be a dolphin professor.

It just slipped out like that, see, before I knew it! I swear I don't know how —"

"I do." Punch shook his head in despair. "You're sure that's all you said?"

"Lord's truth! But I haven't told you the best part, and that's Daddy. He just sat there and said 'dolphin professor' a coupla times. Then he said, 'Skeeter, you'd be real good at that. I don't see how we can manage a college education, but we'll study on it if that's what you want.'

"See what I mean? *We'll study on it.* That's just what he said!" Skeeter bounced on his seat.

"Cool," said Tom. "Now all you need is the money."

Skeeter nodded, full of himself and confidence.

Uh-hunh, thought Punch, all we need is the money. Isn't that where we were last week? Still, he made a big okay sign and smiled at Skeeter.

Inside the museum, Skeeter asked for the curator.

"He's out at the moment," said a pleasant-faced lady with short brown hair and light blue eyes. She reminded Punch of his mother. "I can give him a message, though."

Skeeter swore softly, then pasted his smile back on and outlined their mission.

"How wonderful!" she said. "My name is Mrs. Porter and I work with our curator. Your donations should go to the Cape Lookout National Seashore because you found those things on Shackleford, but we can handle that. Perhaps they'll let us do a display here, since a local boy was the discoverer."

As she examined their treasures, Mrs. Porter made all the right sounds of appreciation. She promised they'd hear soon from the curator or the officials at Cape Lookout. "I hope the jewelry and the spoons are worth something for you," she said. "Let us know how the appraisal comes out. Perhaps we can match the offer and keep them.

"We might even have a special exhibit," she went on. "Something about storms and shipwrecks — showing how people try to protect their valuables from nature's destructive forces. These tins were packed so carefully. And the date — 1796 — my heavens. I wonder how many people were lost in the shipwreck that washed these things up?"

"Well, ma'am . . ." Skeeter began naming the ships he knew that had gone down on the Outer Banks.

Punch stepped back a few paces to whisper to Tom. "How are we going to turn him off?"

"Yeah. Our very own battery toy. We'll just have to let him run down. Let's go outside with Mozart."

Eventually, Skeeter came outdoors and marched everyone up Front Street to the jewelry store. They tethered Mozart to another post and told him, "Stay." Mozart's silky gray mustache drooped and he slumped to the sidewalk, resigned.

Inside, Skeeter said with heavy emphasis, "These

thengs are real antiques." He paused dramatically before giving a brief account of their discovery, concluding with "So acourse we want an appraisal. How soon can we find out?"

The short, pale man behind the counter peered down through his jeweler's glass at the chain and then at the brooches before looking up. "These are old, all right," he said. "I'll take your names now, and complete descriptions of each item. We send antiques up to the Raleigh-Durham area, to the fellow who does our appraisals."

"How long does it take?" pressed Skeeter.

"Three, four weeks maybe. We'll call you."

Skeeter slapped the counter in frustration. "Can you tell us anytheng? About the chain maybe?"

"Oh, it's a good gold chain. Could be worth a lot."

"Several hundred dollars maybe?"

"I believe so." The jeweler smiled in sympathy. "It's hard to wait, I know, but I promise we'll call you."

Punch thought, So it really is a start, just as Skeeter said. We did it! He turned to Tom and they shook hands — blister-covered hands.

Since Punch and Tom would be back home when the appraisal came in, they gave Skeeter's name and phone number, and left the shop. Outside, they jumped up and down and pounded each other. Mozart whimpered and danced around them in shared rejoicing.

"Come on," Punch said. "Ice cream, my treat."

Double-dip cones in hand, they went to sit on the docks, dangling their legs over the water as they watched the varied crafts inch into and out of boat slips in the small port. Punch set Mozart's bowl of vanilla on the grayed planking beside him.

"Did y'all see how I never said anytheng about the metal detector?" Skeeter asked after several big licks of his cone.

Punch stopped licking. True. Skeeter hadn't told the woman at the museum or the jeweler. "Why not?" he asked.

"Yeah, how's come?" said Tom.

"Well, Daddy told me it was against the law to use the detector like we're doin'. It's okay to scoot it over the sand on Atlantic Beach — that's just a regular public beach — but not for treasure huntin', 'specially not in National Seashore places."

Punch sat up straight. "You mean we could get in trouble with the police?"

Skeeter's aqua eyes looked into Punch's deep brown ones and he smiled. "Probably not real trouble, nah. Police round here don't do much at night anyhow. Nothin' ever happens here at night."

Tom crunched his sugar cone and said, "Then why worry? Seems like a dumb law to me. You can't tell people not to hunt for treasure with the best tool there is. That's dopey."

Punch agreed. It seemed hopeless to make laws about things people were going to do anyway, such as as running in the school hallways. And besides, Skeeter needs this treasure, he thought, taking a determined bite of his cone. It's just wasted hidden away somewhere. That's *really* dopey!

And here I am, he realized, worrying about money again. Just now he had spent a week's allowance in the ice cream shop. It was okay. He had wanted to. But if a little ice cream cost so much, what would a college education cost?

We sure can't quit, he decided. We have to go to Hammock House, we just have to, and we can't go in the daytime. It has to be dark, when the policemen are in bed.

He pictured himself in the middle of the night, digging in the evil pirate's yard, and he shivered. The sun burned down upon him and he felt cold all over.

Mozart licked his ear, a slobbery, vanilla thank-you. Punch petted him and thought. Mozie. Sure. I'll have Mozie. And Tom. Big, comfortable Tom. Skeeter, too, of course. That stupid treasure's just sitting somewhere, waiting.

"Punch? You in some kinda trance?" asked Skeeter.

Tom gave a short laugh. "Nah. He's thinking about Hammock House. Right, mumble-mind?" He jabbed Punch in the ribs with a knowing elbow.

"Yeah, I guess we better start tonight and —"

"Tonight?" Skeeter cried. "Y'all are crazy! You thenk I'm gonna go near that place at night? And what if the owner's home?"

Punch nodded. "If he's home, we can't, of course, but the place looks all closed up to me, so I think he's gone. Anyhow,we have to go in the dark when no one'll see us. It's illegal. You just said so. Especially in some historic place like Blackbeard's yard."

Of course, no one wanted to think about being in Blackbeard's yard at night, and they weren't ready to talk about it, either. They boated back up Taylor's Creek to the Wagners', told Punch's family what they had learned in town, and got busy barbecuing hamburgers for lunch.

In the afternoon they set out in the boat again. They talked about everything except what was really on their minds, sharing the binoculars as they looked for the dolphins. They counted the foals in the wild horse herd while they cruised the length of Carrot Island.

No one said any of the dangerous words like "ghost" or "treasure" or "Hammock House." Punch wanted to talk about the small, mysterious skull, but he didn't dare. If Skeeter heard about it, he'd never go near the pirate's house.

As they rounded the western end of the island, Punch saw the glistening silver backs arching upward in the water. "There," he said. "Let her drift, Skeeter."

"Ay, ay, cap'n. Y'all watch the water now, hear? If it gets kinda light-colored, we're driftin' into shaller water. Don't let us run aground." With that, he slipped over the side as smoothly as oil.

94

"How'd you do that?" Tom asked, leaning over-board. "We didn't even rock!"

"I been doin' it ever day, that's how," he said, grinning up at them — a pale, slim seal. He turned away, breast-stroking effortlessly. A few feet into the channel he stopped and treaded water while he squeaked and whistled.

Sweetheart raised her head and squeaked back, then disappeared. In seconds, she burst out of the water in front of Skeeter, who laughed and took hold of one flipper. "Let's go," he said, shifting his hand up onto her dorsal fin.

Punch and Tom watched, awed, as Sweetheart tore through the water with Skeeter — the boy as wild and free as the dolphin. Around the boat they went, swooping up and down in the water as twin undulations — one a slender straw, the other a silver crescent. Both were smiling. One laughed every so often; the other gave a joyous "Eeeee!"

Punch was filled with admiration . . . and envy. Why should only Skeeter have dolphins as playmates? Yet as he watched, he admitted that few boys could do what Skeeter was doing now. It must have been really scary the first few times, he decided.

When the entire school swam over to view the proceedings, Skeeter let go of Sweetheart, rubbing his face against hers — brother caressing sister. He swam back to the boat, vaulting up and in as skillfully as he had left.

"That's some act," Punch said, admiration winning out. "When do you breathe?"

Skeeter giggled, enjoying the glory. "You gotta be quick, for sure. Now, y'all didn't see this, hear? Daddy thenks I do all my checkin' from the boat. I better do it now, too. I haven't been very good since y'all came."

His check on the dolphin school took some time. He named each animal that glided alongside, patting them all lovingly and slipping overboard if he spotted something new or unusual such as a mark in the skin.

"This one's Big Daddy," he said. "The professors say he's real, real old and he's got lotsa scars. See his left flipper? It's in bad shape, but he just won't give up."

Punch watched Skeeter work, and much as he wanted to get in the water, he was intimidated by the large school. I'm their friend, he thought, but they don't know that. He longed to hang on to a flipper and fly through the water like Skeeter . . . except that he knew more now. It wouldn't be that simple. Skeeter's demonstration had required great skill.

The dolphins tired of Skeeter's inspection before he did and left, squeaking and whistling to each other, heading north, repeating their pattern.

"Shoot," Punch said. "I could watch them leap up in the air all day long."

Tom said, "Yeah. I thought people taught them to do that."

"Nah," Skeeter said scornfully. "They thenk it's fun

to jump up and down." He grew thoughtful then. "But it might be hard teachin' 'em to do it when you want 'em to — 'specially in a little, bitty tank where they don't belong."

"We'd better head back," Punch said. "Mom'll be getting hyper again." And we have plans to make, he thought. I don't care how spooky that place is, I'm going to hunt there. We have to.

He tried to put this feeling of certainty into his voice when he said to Skeeter, "What time do you want to meet us at Hammock House?"

"Never. I already told you that."

"It's next on our list," Punch said.

Skeeter's face took on a strange, unreadable expression. "Look here," he began, "I know what you're tryin' to do for me and I'm glad — I mean, it's really somethin' and I know that — but we can't dig up Blackbeard's yard! We just can't!"

He leaned earnestly toward Punch. "How about we hunt all those little islands? They're on our list, too, and they're fine places to hunt, no lie!"

Punch shook his head. "That'll take forever, and it's not as logical. We have to do it right. So I'm going — even if I have to go alone."

Tom looked up from a long contemplation of his knees. With obvious reluctance he said, "Count me in."

9.
Hammock House at Night

"Sure is bright out here," Tom said, eyeing a wispy cloud as it drifted across the nearly full moon. "What if somebody's at Hammock House, Punch? What'll we say?"

"I'm pretty sure it's closed up." Punch shifted the spade to a more comfortable place on his shoulder. "If a neighbor sees us we could say . . . well . . . 'The owner said we could hunt here if we put all the sod back.' How's that?"

Tom stopped walking. "That's the dumbest lie I ever heard." He rested his spade on the sidewalk. "Hold on. I'm thinking."

Punch leaned against a lamppost and waited. Maybe a good lie would present itself if he could concentrate, but he couldn't. He reached out to pat Mozart, who was sitting beside him. Touching him helped.

At least he didn't have to worry about his parents' finding out. Even though it was now only ten-thirty, they were asleep. All the fresh air and exercise sent them to bed early, or so they said.

And Lila was out with her new friends, as she had been nearly every night. He would have to be careful about her, though. She had a way of finding out what he was doing.

The big worry was the pirate's yard, dark and brooding like Blackbeard himself.

"Hey," Tom said in the silence.

Punch jumped and his spade clattered to the sidewalk. "Don't do that, mouse-mind!"

Unruffled, Tom went on. "Isn't that somebody we know?" He pointed down the street to the corner, where a small figure sat, hunched over and very still.

"Right," Punch said, retrieving his spade. He put it on his shoulder like a musket and marched forward. "Let's go."

As they came closer, Skeeter waved and stood up. "This's purely crazy," he said by way of greeting. He had a spade in one hand and the metal detector in the other.

"Yeah, but we can't go on till we're sure it isn't here," Punch insisted. "We made a list so we could do it right and we're doing it. Now come on."

At night Hammock Lane was a place of shadows. The few houses were dark — no windows casting friendly squares of light on the silent lawns. As if in a cemetery, the boys moved warily toward Hammock House until they stood only a few feet from the front porch.

"Are we sure nobody's home?" whispered Tom.

Skeeter nodded. "I asked around. The man that lives here is gone somewhar. Ghosts probly scared him off."

"Don't say that!" said Punch. "We can't even think about it! Anyway, ghosts just . . . just . . ."

"Go, 'Boo!' " finished Tom, his voice oddly high-pitched.

"Very funny," Punch retorted. "Anyway, that's all they do. They go 'Oo-ooo' and flap around but they can't *do* anything. They're just —"

"Evil spirits," Skeeter muttered.

"Forget it," said Punch. "Think about the treasure and think about being a professor at the marine lab."

Momentarily squelched, Skeeter nodded.

In total silence, with Punch and Mozart leading, they edged around the house and into the backyard. Here, moonlight filtered through the oak leaves and lay in pale, wavering patches on the dark grass. The strangely cool air had become a cold night dampness.

Punch gripped Mozart's leash with an icy hand and walked to the center of the yard, where he tried to gauge how much territory they could explore in the next few hours. Far above him an owl went, "Whooot? Whooot?"

Punch's hand jerked on the leash. A hooting owl meant death, or so Lila said.

"Whooot? Whooot?"

Tom gazed upward at the trees. "I wish he wouldn't do that." He, too, had benefited from Lila's knowledge.

"Forget him," Punch said, trying to sound calm. "Let's dig in that back corner. Nobody'd see us there . . . and we can't keep standing around like this."

"Okay by me." But when Tom planted his spade in the ground, he gasped. "Geez! It sure isn't sand. This hole could take the rest of our vacation."

Skeeter stood still, gripping his tools. "I just know we shouldn't be doin' this," he whispered.

Punch jumped on his spade to force it down a few more inches. "It's hard, all right." He grunted as he lifted a small piece of sod. "Put all the pieces with grass on them in one place. We have to put it back so nobody knows we were here."

"Sshhh," Skeeter hissed, looking all around. When only silence answered, he slowly began to dig next to Punch. He had removed one small square of sod when he stopped. "Don't forget the museum," he said. "They'll want the stuff we don't, like bloody clothes, skeletons —"

Tom laid a heavy hand on Skeeter's shoulder. "Not right now, okay?"

"Yeah," Punch agreed, breathing heavily. "Quit messing around, you guys, and dig."

Within minutes, they all had to stop and pull off shirts soaked with perspiration. "Good thing it's cold back here," Tom said, slapping at a mosquito.

Punch thought the cold was creepy. He was pouring sweat and freezing at the same time. He carved out one square of sod after another and cursed Blackbeard with every spadeful. When a breeze drifted through the yard, he shivered all over.

"What's that?" cried Skeeter.

Punch quit digging. "What's what?"

Then he heard it. A rattling sound up at the house. Wood whacking gently against wood, perhaps? Followed by stillness. And again, *whack — whacketa-whack-whack*.

He whispered, "Just the shutters, I think. The wind's making them hit the house."

"It hasn't got any shutters!" whimpered Skeeter.

"He's right," Tom said, leaning on his shovel and staring at the moonlit house.

Punch wiped the sweat on his face and made himself look at the house, which he'd been ignoring successfully until now. No shutters. "Okay. Maybe that porch door's loose."

Whack — whacketa-whack — whack-whack.

"Hrrrr," growled Mozart, ears pointing forward.

Skeeter sidled over by Tom. "I don't see that door movin'," he quavered. "Anyhow, thar's no wind."

"Breeze, then," said Punch. "I felt it before. Just ignore it and keep digging."

His face sorrowful, Skeeter bent over his spade. "Now I lay me down to sleep," he whispered. "Unnh," as he lifted out a full spade. "I pray the Lord my soul — "

Punch looked at Tom and grinned, the grin fading

as they heard it again, a soft, insistent sound that was much too close. *Whack — whacketa-whack — whack*.

"Hrrr," went Mozart, louder. He looked around at Punch, as if waiting for him to do something. Punch patted him and said, "Hurry up, you guys. The hole will be deep enough to test pretty soon."

All of them dug frantically for several minutes, heaping the heavy clods on all sides of the growing pit. Punch groaned and complained as he hefted each load, hoping to drown out all other sound. Even so, Skeeter's prayerful chant and the eerie rattle of Hammock House beat insistently on his nerves.

"Stop," he said. "We're a couple of feet down and it's plenty big. Try the detector."

Skeeter moved the detector across every inch of their pit. No cheerful *beep, beep*. All they heard was *whack — whacketa — whack* from the house.

"Y'all thenk that sound's gettin' closer?" Skeeter asked as he climbed out of the hole.

Convinced that there had to be a logical reason for the noise, Punch examined the house. What he saw made him stiffen with fear. "There," he breathed, pointing to a second-story window.

"I don't see any —" Tom began. Then, "Oh, yeah. You mean the curtains?"

All three looked at the window, clearly visible in the moonlight. Curtains hung down on either side of the glass panes, but those on the right swayed inward a trifle, then back to the side. A few seconds later, they drifted toward the center again, eddying to and fro before slipping back to the window's edge.

"It's the breeze," Punch said, knowing it wasn't.

"The windows are closed, mini-mind," said Tom.

Skeeter picked up his spade. "I'm not sayin' the word, y'all, but that's a you-know-what and I'm goin' home."

Tom started piling dirt back into the pit. "Maybe it's been doing that all along. We didn't look up there before."

Mmhmm, thought Punch, but what if something's inside? Something that threw that little skull at me, maybe? What if it's making that sound and moving the curtains, too? He didn't dare voice any of those thoughts, of course.

Out loud he said, "We're okay, you know. Nothing's happened — not really. Let's just throw the dirt in and put the sod on. We can fix it nice next time." Recklessly, he hurled dirt at the pit.

"Next time, my Aunt Fanny!" cried Skeeter. "You know any other house acts like this? Nossir, boy! That's 'cause this one's haunted!" As he threw clods back into the gaping hole, Skeeter alternated curses with bits of prayer.

As soon as they finished, Tom jumped up and down on the dirt and they topped it with sod.

"Looks okay to me," Punch said.

"That curtain's movin' again. I'm gone!" Before

104

Punch could say anything, Skeeter vanished, slipping through the hedges into the night.

"It's only midnight, for crum's sake," grumbled Punch. "We could've dug at least one more hole."

"The crew jumped ship, Captain." Tom handed Punch his spade. "Let's go home. I could drink about six Cokes."

Seeming as eager to leave as Skeeter, Mozart pulled back toward the lighted street with all his strength. His behavior unnerved Punch. Why, he wondered, would his dog feel such a powerful need to leave this yard?

Because it was nearly two before Punch and Tom fell asleep, they slept late the next morning. They might have slept even later, but at ten o'clock Mrs. Wagner called upstairs. "Punch? Get up, please. The museum director is on the phone for you."

The voice on the other end of the line was hearty, full of gratitude and congratulations. "We're going to share ownership of your find with the Cape Lookout folks," the director explained, "because it was found in their territory.

"You may not know it, being from out of state, but we have an untold amount of treasure buried in these parts," he went on. "Blackbeard's, of course, is the most tempting. If you and your friends are interested, stop by my office someday. I've had my eye on one of the smaller islands north of here for some time, and

I can't think of anyone I'd rather have find it than a group of boys."

"Thanks," Punch said, now fully awake. "Thanks a lot! We'll sure do that. Don't tell anyone else about that island, okay?"

Back in their room, he told Tom about the phone call. "Yahoo!" Tom exulted. "Pieces of eight, you bet!"

"Yeah, and you guys said I was crazy." But the museum director didn't think so, and he ought to know, Punch thought as he rummaged in his drawer for clean shorts. His hand bumped the tiny skull and he recoiled as if he'd been burned.

Come on, he scolded himself. It's a junky little piece of plastic. I should pitch it and forget it. He imagined the skull's beady red eyes glittering at him, and his hand closed around it, but in the end, he shoved the skull into its corner and slammed the drawer shut.

When Skeeter drifted in at noon, Punch led him upstairs where they could talk. Lila's eyes followed them, but she didn't say anything. He would have to tell her something before long — but not about Hammock House, he decided. She'd go into her ghost and haunted house routine and he couldn't take it. She was too convincing.

"Called me, too," said Skeeter when he heard about Punch's phone call. "Nice man. He told me about that little island, too. It's kinda far away, but I thenk we should go. No point in waitin'."

The argument that ensued was conducted in whispers so no one would overhear, but it was heated nonetheless. The words "purely stupid" and "muleheaded Yankee" occurred often.

"Oh, all right," Skeeter said, yielding at last. "But it's a full moon tonight and we're gonna hear that poor French girl, Lord's truth. I reckon that's what it's gonna take to get us outa thar for good."

"Boys," came Mrs. Wagner's voice, "come on down. We're ready to leave for the aquarium."

In the car, Skeeter thanked Punch's mom for including him, saying that the aquarium was one of his favorite places. "Ever one a my classes comes here," he explained on the way. "I can do the whole tour, just in case our guide leaves somethin' out."

By ten-thirty that Tuesday night, the boys and Mozart were back in Blackbeard's yard. At first they were tense, dreading the mysterious sounds of the previous night.

Skeeter leaned on his spade and stared at the house. "I don't hear a theng," he said after several minutes. "That curtain isn't movin' either."

Punch carved out another square of sod. "There isn't any wind. Must have something to do with wind. Dig, Skeeter! We don't want to be here all night."

"Sure is hard work," said Tom, panting as he piled squares of sod beside the hole. "But it's better tonight. Even Mozart thinks so."

Punch glanced at his dog, resting on the grass with his nose on his paws. Last night he had been alert every second, emitting frequent growls at the house.

Punch began humming "This Land Is Your Land," an old Woody Guthrie tune they had heard earlier in the evening when they had sat on the deck, visiting with Skeeter's dad. Punch liked Guthrie's music and Mr. Grace. Both made him feel good.

Lila's music — and his dad's — on the other hand, usually put him to sleep. And he couldn't sing along with any of their pieces. If those songs have words, he thought, I'll bet they're pretty sappy.

Contentedly he sang, ". . . from the Gulf Stream waters . . ." — interspersing words of the song with hearty grunts as he piled dirt next to the squares of sod.

"Hrrr," said Mozart, now on his feet, staring at the house. "Hrrr." His lip curled upward to reveal his teeth.

Everyone stopped digging. Skeeter moved from his side of the pit to stand between Punch and Tom.

Punch forced himself to look at Hammock House in the light of the moon, now fully round. It shone at an angle on the back of the house, illuminating some of the windows and leaving others as dark, blank panes.

"On the right, upstairs," whispered Tom.

Punch felt himself grow cold all over as he watched the deeply shadowed window. Behind the panes, from somewhere in that room, a light moved back and forth.

108

It wavered as a candle might, then came nearer and nearer to the window.

"It's her," Skeeter quavered, clutching Punch's elbow.

"Rraarf!" yelped Mozart.

Instantly the light disappeared and the window went dark.

"Whoever it is heard Mozart," Tom whispered.

Punch scoured his brain for a good, scientific reason to explain the eerie light in the house.

"Nnnn," moaned Skeeter as his fingers dug into Punch's arm. "Look downstairs. She's thar, sure as you're born."

Punch looked and there it was! The light had moved downstairs, just as Skeeter said. Punch stood immobile now, feeling the first stabs of real fear. His throat was so tight he couldn't make a sound.

As they stood there — all of them nailed to the ground in terror — a tortured, unearthly scream filled the night and Blackbeard's yard.

10•

Is It Blackbeard?

The ghoulish shriek lingered in the night, triumphing over all other sound, paralyzing their minds and bodies until, with agonizing slowness, it faded into the dark. In a primeval response, Mozart threw back his head and howled.

Only then were the boys able to move. They took off running, bounding over the spiky plants at the side of the yard, leaving spades and metal detector behind in their haste. Beside Punch ran Mozart, his leash whipping the ground as it lashed up and down.

"Down thar!" cried Skeeter, pointing to a corner.

They raced down the sidewalks, heedless of tricycles forgotten after play and the jagged, uneven sections of pavement. Gradually Skeeter slowed to a jog, which subsided to a jerky walk after several blocks.

"Bet we set . . . a record for the . . . eight-hundred-meter run," Tom panted.

"Where are we?" Punch pressed one hand into his left side, cramped in pain from the mad dash.

"My place," said Skeeter. "Coupla houses more. We'll sit on the back stoop whar we can talk."

Skeeter's part of town was old, its houses small and close together. Ancient live oaks arched above the lawns, bestowing welcome shade and a stately permanence on life. Lamplight shone from a few windows and laughter broke the stillness now and then.

Punch sank onto the cement stoop and leaned back against the Graces' house, feeling the last of its daytime warmth seep into his body. He was silent, eyes closed. At his feet, Mozart panted noisily.

Tom pointed a shaky finger at Skeeter. "One point for you. That house is *haunted!*"

"I'm sure sorry," Skeeter replied in a small voice. "But Wally told me. When the moon's full, she screams. Like to scared me right outa my pants."

Punch tried to think of something hopeful to say and gave up. "Those spades belong to our rented house. We have to go back and get them."

"Not now!" chorused Tom and Skeeter.

"Don't sweat it," Skeeter added. "Nobody ever goes near that place. That stuff is safe, no lie."

"Okay, okay," Punch answered wearily. He leaned forward, elbows on his knees, hands supporting his chin. I never did like horror stories or creepy movies, he thought, and now I'm *living* one. Hoo-ee.

As Punch calmed down, his mind began to work in its old, logical way. His brain seethed with questions. Are ghosts real? Is some restless spirit living at Ham-

111

mock House? Can a murdered person really come back and make screams like that? Was it that French girl or someone else?

Abruptly he asked, "Who do you think screamed?"

"That poor French girl, acourse," said Skeeter.

"Blackbeard," Tom said decisively. "It was a man — a really, really angry man. I never heard anybody that mad."

"Either way, it's a ghost," Skeeter declared, "and I'm not goin' back thar. I'd ruther pound nails and saw boards *all my life* than go back thar."

Punch watched his face and thought, he doesn't mean that. He's just scared now, like me and Tom.

"Does the ghost scream all the time," Punch asked, "or just when the moon's full?"

"I reckon mainly when the moon's full . . . but you don't thenk we should —"

"Don't worry," Punch said soothingly, "but we left our spades there, so —"

"My detector!" cried Skeeter. "Only it's Daddy's, really. Hang it all, anyhow —"

"Right," Punch said, trying to sound calmer than he felt. "We'll figure out a way to get that stuff back. We can wear garlic around our necks or big crosses — you know."

Tom snorted. "Garlic's for werewolves or vampires."

"There must be something that scares ghosts, too," Punch insisted. "We'll ask Lila. Just relax, you guys."

Punch looked anxiously from Tom to Skeeter, hoping he had quieted their fears. They had to retrieve the spades as well as the Graces' metal detector, no question about that. But Punch wanted to be the one to decide when and how.

"Let's head out," Tom said, standing up, "I could use some sack time." He grinned. "This vacation is hard work."

"Yeah," Skeeter said. "I don't want to even thenk about this ever again. Here I got my hopes up and now —" He broke off and raked one hand through his hair, all the while avoiding their eyes.

Uh-hunh, thought Punch, I was right. He didn't mean what he said before. "Hey," he said to Skeeter. "We aren't quitting. That treasure's out there and we're going to find it, okay? But it's late now. We'll see you tomorrow."

Sneaking back into the house was as easy as sneaking out had been earlier. Punch and Tom slipped into their beds without talking. Punch knew Tom hoped never to see Hammock House again and he didn't blame him. I probably wouldn't go back either, he thought, if it weren't for Skeeter.

He fell asleep thinking of Skeeter as he had last seen him — downcast, one hand sadly combing the sun-bleached hair. Punch didn't understand how he had come to adopt this straw boy, but he had . . . and there was no going back.

113

The next morning, Punch followed Lila outdoors to the deck when she went there to practice. "Uh, Lila," he began, praying for inspiration, not wanting her to know exactly what he and his friends were doing.

"Better hurry up," she said low. "The folks are coming out here with their coffee. What's going on, anyway? Where are you guys hunting now?"

"Well, see, we're sort of in between, but, uh . . . Skeeter's all worried about ghosts. We have to help him chill out, so I was wonder —"

Up went her cello bow, a royal scepter. "Tell me you're not hunting at Hammock House."

Punch managed a weak smile.

"You total dope," she said, pointing the bow straight at him. "You used to *think*, at least now and then! Don't you know that's against the law, and whoever lives there will —"

"Shhh," hissed Punch, one eye on the door to the deck. "Nobody'll ever know we were there. I just need to find out something. Are ghosts afraid of crosses? Are they?"

Lila poked his stomach with her bow. "I don't believe you're really doing this. That place is haunted! Every person in this town knows it's haunted!"

Punch ignored the stabbing bow and persisted. "So that's why I have to find out about crosses, just in case they're right."

Lila withdrew the bow and bent over her cello to

114

tune it. "Mmmm," she hummed, plucking the A string.

"Lila!" urged Punch.

"You can't count on it," she replied cryptically. "Sometimes a cross works. Sometimes it doesn't."

Mrs. Wagner, coffee in hand, came out the deck door. "Oh, good, here you are," she said. "I'm going to sit a bit, then we need everybody's help, okay? The house is a minor disaster."

The next couple of hours were a disaster as far as the boys were concerned. "When I grow up," Punch told Tom, "I'm not cleaning. Not ever."

Skeeter arrived as the family was finishing lunch. "Y'all got big plans for today?" he asked.

"No, Skeeter, we don't," said Punch's mom. "I was about to suggest fishing, but fish don't bite midday, do they?"

"No, ma'am. Night's a lot better, or early mornin'. How'd y'all like to go find the dolphins?"

"Great idea!" said Professor Wagner. "We'd better wear our hats, though. That sun is fierce."

On her way to the boat, Lila ruffled Skeeter's hair. "I'm glad you and your dad live here. This is awfully nice."

Skeeter gazed dreamily after her as she moved toward a seat in the bow.

"Don't get any ideas," Tom said, frowning as he strode past Skeeter.

When everyone was in the Wagners' boat, Skeeter cast off and landed nimbly in the bow beside Lila and behind Mozart, the yapping figurehead. "We can take turns lookin' for the dolphins, Lila," Skeeter said, offering her the binoculars.

Punch saw Tom glaring at Skeeter's back and wondered if his sister knew what she had stirred up. No, he decided, she's clueless. Always has been.

"I don't get it," Skeeter said as time went by. "Scoot over near Pivers Island, Mr. Wagner. We'll try that awhile."

Punch saw them first. "Look where I'm pointing, Mom. See the fins?"

Some distance away, two silver dolphins sailed upward, flipping their tails at the top of the arc before plunging back down into the water.

His mom and dad went "Ohhh."

Punch, too, watched with undiminished awe. He wondered what it would be like to be so coordinated — to fit into your world with such perfection. Lately, growing rapidly in height, he often felt awkward and clumsy. He kept bumping into furniture and doorways he hadn't meant to touch.

But a dolphin moved with exquisite grace — an ideal blend of animal and element. He stretched forth an eager hand as three of the smaller ones approached.

"Now this's more like it," said Skeeter in the tone

116

of an approving father. "Let 'er drift, sir. They'll all come over now."

"Rrarff! Rrarff!" scolded the figurehead.

Skeeter clamped his hands around Mozart's muzzle. "No, no, doggie. Hush yourself, hear?"

Mozart turned his head and whimpered at Punch.

"No barking, Mozie!" Punch ordered.

The dolphins cavorted around the boat, enchanting the people and bedeviling the dog. As Mozart leaned out to stare a dolphin in the eye, it squeaked impudently and splashed water in his face with an unerring flipper before diving under the boat.

Mozart shook off the water and dashed to the other side of the boat. "Hrrr," he growled, leaning over the water, waiting for the big, rude thing to reappear.

Up popped the grinning dolphin. "Eeeee-ee!" Then *splash!* and the dolphin dove out of reach.

Mozart zipped from side to side as the dolphins popped up and down and the people laughed till tears ran down their faces.

"Poor Mozie," gasped Punch's mom when she could talk. "This is the funniest thing I've ever seen."

As before, the dolphins decided when to end the game, swimming off in ones and twos like children straggling into school after recess.

"I could do this every day of my life," Mrs. Wagner said, eyes shaded as she gazed after the last few glistening bodies. Professor Wagner nodded in agreement.

"Does that mean y'all are comin' back next summer?"

"It does," said Punch's father, slapping the boat for emphasis. "Now let's head for town and that ice cream shop."

Late that afternoon, back at the house, Punch took Tom and Skeeter aside. "We have to plan how to get our stuff back," he said.

Skeeter frowned. "The spades are nothin' — it's that danged detector. It cost the world."

"Let's get it over with," Tom said, heading for the front door.

"Nossir." Skeeter stood with his feet apart, planted like a small tree. "Not when folks can see us and not till the moon's done bein' full. Nossir. And I mean it this time, I purely do."

"Okay by me," Punch said. "We'll just be cool a couple days. You're right, you know? We don't dare go back when people could see us."

Inwardly, Punch was exultant. I can't believe he said that! he thought. As soon as he thinks the ghost is gone, we can go back at night. And while we're there . . . His mind hummed with hope again. Of course, Skeeter would need some serious persuading.

That evening, Skeeter and his dad went over to Morehead City with the Wagners for dinner at a waterfront restaurant. Thursday, Mr. Grace took a rare day off to show them some tiny, uninhabited islands

118

with pristine beaches. Each of these nights the moon shone full and round upon the town of Beaufort, or so it seemed to Punch and Tom, who examined it with anxious eyes.

By Friday, Punch was ready to burst. Only two days left! Two measly days . . . and nights.

Well, tonight something had to happen. We'll get real big crosses, he decided. Even a half-blind ghost could see an enormous cross.

"Come on, Tom," he said after breakfast. "I called Skeeter and he's meeting us in town. We're going shopping."

11•
A Dark Shadow

Punch and Tom met Skeeter outside the jewelry store in town, where Mozart greeted Skeeter with approving barks.

Skeeter bent down to hug him, but he was looking at Punch. "You know y'all are purely —" he began.

"I know," Punch interrupted. "But we have to get our stuff back and this's the safest way. Besides, the moon can't still be full after all this time."

Tom grinned at Skeeter and shrugged his shoulders. "You're right. Crazy."

"Did Lila say for sure ghosts are scared of crosses?" Skeeter demanded of Punch.

"Pretty much," he lied. "If we get giant ones, they ought to be good for just about anything. Even vampires are afraid of crosses, and vampires are lots scarier than some wimpy little girl ghost."

"Huh!" Skeeter made a face. "She didn't sound wimpy to me. Did she to you, Tom? You said it was Blackbeard himself! Call *him* wimpy, you'll be deader'n a doornail."

120

Still arguing, they checked the cases in the jewelry store and found nothing suitable. The second shop was larger and more promising. Here, everyday necessities were mixed with postcards, T-shirts, and other tourist souvenirs.

In a case of jewelry, Punch and Tom found large crosses made of pearly shells glued to heavy wooden backs.

"This'll show up great in the moonlight," Tom said, holding one up and twirling it around.

"We can wear real dark sweatshirts," said Punch, thinking also of the strange chill in the pirate's yard. To the listening saleswoman he said, "These are for a church camp-out."

"What a nice idea," she cooed. As she left to ring up their purchase, Tom snorted with laughter and Punch had to sock him in the stomach to shut him up.

Though he insisted he was not coming, Skeeter chose the largest cross in the case, a glittering, hammered-silver extravaganza priced at $9.95.

"It's silver plate, not silver," the clerk told Skeeter.

Skeeter replied formally, "It's for my grandmother. She knows I can't buy real silver. Would y'all giftwrap it, please?"

Tom whispered to Punch, "Is he serious?"

Punch just shook his head.

Back at the house, they hid all three crosses under Punch's pillow and changed into bathing suits for a trip to Carrot Island. As they crossed the narrow waterway, Punch thought, This could be our last trip here. He had stopped talking about their return to Hammock House, as had the others. It was an oddly silent trio that dumped their towels and lunch on the sand under the gnarled cedars.

"I'd better take Mom some sand dollars," Tom said, heading for Bird Shoal.

"Yeah, my mom wants more, too. I'll go with you." Punch followed a few steps after his friend.

"I told Daddy I'd dig clams," Skeeter said. "I'll be your way later."

By late afternoon they had collected sand dollars and clams, eaten their picnic, held underwater swimming races, and roasted marshmallows. As a farewell, Punch fed an entire loaf of bread to the gulls, piece by tiny piece, making the loaf last as long as he could.

Still, like an ominous stage backdrop setting the mood for a play, the darkened yard at Hammock House was never far from his mind.

Back at the house, after they had showered and were changing clothes before dinner, Tom asked, "How soon can we leave? I want to get this over with."

"I'd best be goin'," Skeeter said. "Bye, y'all." He was out of the room and hopping downstairs before either Punch or Tom could reply.

"He left his cross," Punch said, feeling under his pillow. "All three are still here."

"He probably just forgot," Tom said. "We'll take it to him. He'll have to show up to get his detector back."

After dinner, Lila and Professor Wagner tuned their instruments and gave a small concert on the violin and cello outside on the deck. To the music of Vivaldi, the sun sank like a deep pink flower.

"I will never forget this," Punch's mom said, her eyes moist. She reached out to squeeze Punch's hand, then Tom's. "Punch? Punch, are you awake?"

"Hunh? Oh, sure, Mom. Guess it's all this fresh air and exercise. Heh, heh," he added, knowing he sounded as bright as the average gerbil.

Crum, he thought, blinking furiously. How could I just go to sleep like that — when I'm so nervous? I must be falling apart. This treasure-hunting business is a mankiller. No wonder Blackbeard's gold is still hidden.

He leaned around his mother to see what Tom was doing and saw his friend staring blankly out across the water.

At nine that evening, Lila's friends came to pick her up. As she left she waggled her fingers at Punch and Tom. "You guys take care, okay? Don't do anything I wouldn't do."

The door shut behind her, and Professor Wagner turned to Punch. "What do you suppose she meant by that?"

"Oh, it's just a saying," Punch replied, carefully off-hand. "What could we do, anyway? Tom and I are tying flies. Does that look dangerous to you?"

"Odd," muttered his father. "It's not like her to be flippant. Is that part of growing up?" he asked Punch's mom.

Mrs. Wagner stopped writing her postcard. "No, dear, it's not. And Lila is nearly grown up now. You're going to have to face that."

Professor Wagner shook his head. "Not yet." He eyed Punch and Tom. "I suppose you plan to grow up, too, and go away someday."

"Sure, Dad," Punch said, grinning. "All kids do."

"I don't like it," said his father. With a sigh, he picked up his book.

Punch handed a few tiny red feathers to Tom so he could continue with his fly. They worked in silence, Punch thinking about what his dad had said. More and more lately, his father said things that surprised him. I don't know him very well, Punch realized.

Sometime later, his parents warned them not to stay up too late and yawned their way upstairs. The house grew quiet. Unaware of the tension, Mozart dozed on the rug between Punch and Tom.

It wasn't long before Punch put the new flies he had tied into his fish box. He was too jumpy to sit another minute. "Let's get a sandwich," he suggested.

As they sat at the table with peanut butter sand-wiches, Punch said, "We haven't heard a peep for twenty minutes. Soon as we're done, let's pretend to go to bed, just in case anybody's listening. Then we can go, okay?"

And finally they crept away from the house with three crosses and one schnauzer, who panted with excitement at the unexpected late walk.

When they turned left onto Fulford, heading down toward Hammock Lane, they saw him — the same small figure perched on the curb under the streetlight. As they came closer Skeeter rose. "I'm goin' in thar, gettin' it, and then I'm gone. Y'all got that?"

"Look up there," Punch replied, pointing to the moon. "It isn't full anymore, and there's no wind. We'll be fine. Here's your cross, Skeeter. We're putting ours on now."

"I'm tellin' y'all, I'm gettin' the detector and then I'm gone." But he took the gift box. He methodically removed the bow, the gold sticker, and the paper and tucked all of it into his hip pocket.

"If I live through this, I'm givin' this cross to Mamaw."

"Hey, we're nervous enough!" Tom said.

Punch felt more comfortable when he saw how prominent the crosses were against everyone's dark sweatshirts. A ghost would have to think twice before tangling with such an obviously holy trio. Skeeter's silver faceted cross covered his entire chest.

Punch gripped Mozart's leash and took them forward, down Hammock Lane to Hammock House, across the front yard, and around the yaupon bushes with never a faltering step. He glanced over his shoulder at the house and saw nothing. It was a white, two-story building with darkened windows and no sign of life whatsoever.

"Well, now that we're here . . ." Punch began.

Skeeter shook his head violently. "No way! Y'all can just forget it."

"Look around," Punch pleaded. "Do you see or hear anything at all? Anything? It's gone, I tell you. And *we're all here.* We could dig one more nice hole to be sure — just as long as we don't hear anything weird — just for a few minutes!"

Tom moved over to the hole they had abandoned the night of the horrifying scream. "We had a great start here," he said. "Wouldn't take much."

Punch bent down and picked up his spade. "Yeah, and I'm going to dig. It's too good a chance to pass up. We have to go home in a couple days."

Skeeter stamped the ground. "And if I take my detector, then what?"

"Then me and Tom keep all the treasure." Punch grinned.

"Come on, Skeeter," Tom said. "Just a few minutes. Just till we check out this hole."

"I never," Skeeter began, then stopped and stamped the ground again. "Okay, okay! But if a little bitty leaf so much as wiggles . . ." He picked up his spade and began to dig, his eyes fixed on the house, not the excavation.

Heartened, Punch dug strongly down into the ground that long ago had felt the heavy footsteps of Blackbeard and his men. Like Skeeter, he kept watch on the house.

But tonight no curtains moved in the windows of Hammock House. And nothing made repeated *whack-whack* sounds to alarm them.

"Okay, Skeeter," he said before long. "Looks big enough to me. Go ahead and test."

Skeeter began his survey with the metal detector and Tom moved next to Punch. Tom dripped with perspiration and rubbed one sweatshirted arm across his face. "I didn't hit a thing where I was," he said. "I don't think we'll hear any nice *beep, beep* from this hole."

When this gloomy prophecy was proved right, they filled in the hole, stamped it flat, and replaced the sod. Throughout, they cast anxious glances at the house that loomed so uncomfortably near.

"It's not even midnight," Punch said. "I'm going to dig over here near this tree stump. People always bury stuff under trees, remember? Bet we should have started here."

"And then that's it!" Skeeter said, glaring first at Punch, then at Tom. "This is the last hole, Lord's truth."

"We'll leave after this," Punch said. "We'll have checked out enough, don't you think, Tom?"

"Shhh," warned Skeeter, wrestling with a tree root and eyeing the house at the same time.

"What if we find bones?" Tom asked. "This could be the tree they hanged her from — where they buried her."

"Mnnnnn," whined Mozart, who crouched nearby.

Punch stopped digging and looked at his dog. Nose and ears quivering, Mozart was staring at the house. In slow motion he rose to his feet, his stubby tail rigid, his body pointing at the pirate's house.

The perspiration on Punch's skin turned ice-cold as he viewed the house. Downstairs, where no light had been before, wavered a thin, unsteady beam, almost undetectable through the enclosed back porch.

Someone was inside the house.

Clink, clink. It was a faint, metallic sound.

"Hrrr." Mozart's lip curled in a snarl.

"What's wrong?" asked Tom, peering at the upstairs windows.

"There." Punch nodded at the porch. He stood facing it so that his cross would be clearly visible.

Clink, clink, clink. It was very clear this time, definitely something metal.

"That's a chain!" Skeeter wailed as he clutched his cross. "Pirates are always puttin' people in chains."

"Let's get out of here!" Tom cried. Still he watched — as they all did — frozen in place by their fear.

The door to the porch opened and an enormous dark shadow moved into the yard. With it came the light, which appeared to float in midair about four feet off the ground.

"Run!" Punch ordered. "Come on, Mozie!"

They had managed only a few steps when a voice thundered, "Avast, ye villains! Halt where ye are or this cutlass o' mine will have ye for breakfast!"

Paralyzed by the shadow's voice, Punch stood as still as a boy of stone. Skeeter dropped to the ground, whimpering pitifully. Tom turned and raised his spade to strike.

Now it stood in the faint moonlight, no longer a shadow but a giant of a man. Atop his head sat a tri-cornered hat and across his chest, like an unholy wound, ran a blood-red sash laced with shining pistols and daggers.

The hand holding the candle had a long chain draped over its arm. The other arm, raised high, held the sharp, deadly cutlass.

But it was the full, braided black beard that told them their luck had run out. The treasure hunt was over.

12•
The Beaufort Pirate

Brandishing his cutlass, the fearsome pirate strode toward them.

"Rrarrff! Rrarrff! Rrarrff!" Mozart's entire body shook with the fury of his barking.

Punch dropped to his knees beside him. "No, Mozie, no," he begged, almost sobbing. "You'll make him madder."

"Ye swine!" roared the huge pirate, now only a few feet away. "What do ye think ye're doing? Digging ground that does not belong to ye!" Feet planted far apart, he pointed his cutlass at Tom.

"Drop that spade! Ye don't think ye can fight me with that puny thing, do ye now?" He roared obscenely, belly jiggling with laughter at his own humor.

"Hrrr," rumbled Mozart, his fur standing on end.

As he clutched Mozie's collar, Punch could feel his heart thumping in his chest, but his mind was no longer paralyzed. Ghosts don't have big jiggly stomachs, he thought. And the real Blackbeard is dead.

131

Lieutenant Maynard hacked off his head and jammed it on his bowsprit.

In a weak, thready voice not at all his own, Punch said, "You can't be Blackbeard. He's dead."

"Are ye so sure now?" boomed the pirate, rattling his chain and thrashing his cutlass in the air.

Skeeter recovered enough to begin mumbling, "Our Father, who art in Heaven . . ."

"Aye!" bawled the giant. "Ye had better pray!"

Tom sidled over toward Punch. "Yeah," he said, his voice as thin as Punch's. "Who are you, anyway?"

Abruptly, the pirate lowered his cutlass and rested it against one leg so that he could adjust his bushy mustache. He sneezed violently.

"Ah, well," he said, itching his nose, "it was fun while it lasted. Scared you silly, though, didn't I? Betcha peed your pants good, you little devils. Now tell me who *you* are!"

Skeeter stopped praying and stared.

Punch took a shaky breath and stood up. "We aren't from here," he said, his voice gaining strength, "so it doesn't make any difference who we are. We were just looking for Blackbeard's treasure. We'll fix the yard."

"Just looking for treasure? By God, boy, every treasure hunter under the sun has dug up this yard! This's the best-cultivated plot of land in all North Carolina! Didn't anyone tell you that?" Again, he roared with laughter, making the pistols and daggers bounce up and down on his stomach.

Punch sagged under the heavy voice of truth. No one had told him because he had kept their hunt a secret from everyone except Lila. And how would she have known?

Wearily he said, "No, no one told us. This is all my fault — right from the beginning. I'm very sorry about the mess, but I promise we'll fix it."

"I'll be —" muttered Skeeter, cursing with feeling, though in a very soft voice.

The gigantic pirate considered Punch from under bushy black eyebrows, which must have itched like his nose, for he reached up and detached each one. He tucked them in his pocket, then rubbed his own white eyebrows reflectively.

"Well, lads," he said, blowing out the candle, "I'm sorry for you then. You didn't know. I can see you've worked hard back here, too. As a friend of the owner, though, I'm counting on you to make it right."

"Ah," breathed Punch, beginning to see. "So you play the part of Blackbeard to guard the property when the owner's gone."

"I do." He removed his pirate hat and unhooked the thick, braided beard from his ears where it had been anchored. "It's a bit of a joke we have, he and I. I do Blackbeard off and on, in pageants and historical plays hereabouts, so I have the hang of it pretty well."

Punch looked at Tom and Skeeter and they nodded. Yes, he had the hang of it all right. Punch had never been so frightened. He had wet his pants, too, just as the man had said. He wondered if Tom and Skeeter had.

Tom sat down on the ground, folding his legs Indian style. "So you made the curtains move and that weird little *whack-whack* sound a few nights ago?" he asked.

"Not me," the man said, sitting down himself. "Wind does that. When it's just right, it sets the shingles on the roof to flapping and it whuffs down those chimneys and riles the curtains."

"And . . . the scream?" ventured Skeeter. "Y'all do a really great scream. I'll betcha thought that'd scare us off for sure."

The man pursed his lips and frowned. "When did you hear that scream?"

"Tuesday night. Reckon it was near midnight, right, Punch?"

"Yes," Punch replied, his eyes on the man's face.

The old man shook his head. "Nossir. I was home in Morehead City that night — all night. It was the next day I noticed some damfool people — pardon me — had been here digging again. That's when I got my costume ready."

The boys exchanged looks. That unearthly shriek, once heard, could never be forgotten.

"Well, *somebody* screamed," Punch said. "It was the creepiest sound I ever heard. Who do you think did that?"

The man leaned forward. "Hammock House has several ghosts, boy. No one can explain it — but you

134

heard for yourself. Now come on," he said, wheezing as he heaved his bulk upward. "We all belong in bed. Tomorrow, you repair the yard and we're square."

They said good-bye, and Punch, Tom, and Mozart walked Skeeter partway home. On the way, Punch got a faint taste of blood in his mouth and knew that fear had made him chew up his own cheek. His tongue explored the small wounded place and he was quiet, thinking.

At his corner, Skeeter said, "I'm not for certain, but I thenk my har turned white. I was sure we were gonna die, all hacked into little-bitty pieces like crow's meat. I did pee my pants, too, just like a baby. Y'all sure know how to have excitin' vacations." He grinned at Punch.

"Tomorra," he went on, "let's go find the dolphins and forget this ever happened."

"We aren't ever going to forget," Tom said.

Punch smiled back at Skeeter, who hadn't said "I told you so" or reminded him of how dumb it had been to insist on hunting at Hammock House. The guys at home would like this kid a lot. "Hey, Skeeter," he said, "take the cross off before you go in the house."

Punch and Tom were tiptoeing upstairs in their own house when someone flipped on the hall light above them.

"Boys?" asked Professor Wagner in his night voice, soft and husky. "Why are you up? It's after one o'clock."

Punch tried to think of a wonderful, logical lie and he couldn't. He was all wrung out. Instead, he sat down on the steps and put his head in his hands.

Tom nudged him with a warning foot and said, "Well, see, Professor, it was so nice out we decided, you know, since we're going home soon and we'll really miss this place . . . well, we thought —"

Punch's father came to where they were stranded on the steps. "A most heroic effort, Tom, but rather thin in substance. Let's go to the kitchen where we can talk."

Silently, Punch and Tom went into the kitchen and sat down at the table. Mozart looked from one human to the other as if to say, *You are all confused,* and then trotted upstairs alone. Professor Wagner poured lemonade and set a box of crackers on the table.

When he sat down he said to Punch, "I don't bite, you know. If it's something you're ashamed of, you'll feel better if you tell someone."

Punch found he was ready to talk. Eager, in fact.

"Dad," he began, "I had this terrific idea in the car on the way down here. . . ."

Some time later, when the lemonade and crackers were gone, Punch finished with, "And it was super dumb. I didn't even check to see if Blackbeard's yard had been dug up before and because of me we all nearly croaked —"

"No we didn't," Tom interrupted, speaking for the first time. "We agreed to hunt there when we made our list. I'd put my treasure there if I was Black-beard."

Professor Wagner absently stroked the few strands of hair meandering across his bald spot. "Yes, but the whole thing was rather headlong — a trifle impetuous." He began to smile as he went on.

"You may find this hard to believe, but as kids, Lanky and I spent years looking for that treasure. Had a wonderful time doing it, too. God only knows where the man hid it, but he may have buried it for all eternity."

Tom sat up suddenly and pointed at Professor Wagner. "You put that book on Beaufort in the car. You knew we'd find out about Blackbeard, huh?"

"Smart boy," he replied, with a nod for Tom.

"You mean you dug at Hammock House, too?" Punch asked. Like me? was his unspoken thought. For the first time he looked at his dad and wondered how much they were alike.

"No, not there. Lanky knew it'd been dug to death, as it were." He rose and took the glasses to the sink.

"Punch, quit feeling bad now. You and Tom learned more about yourselves in these two weeks than most people learn in ten normal years. And you did find treasure, though maybe not the kind you were looking for."

He paused, one hand on the light switch. "I know I saddled you with Skeeter without much forethought. But look what came of it. Funny thing, life, isn't it?"

Punch sat still, agreeing, but dreading the lecture to come. A lecture I deserve, he thought.

His father flicked the switch and they were in the dark. "Let's go to bed, you guys. Next time, Punch, just run any terrific ideas by me, okay?"

Saturday morning everyone packed suitcases and tidied the house before enjoying their final afternoon of vacation. As he was emptying his dresser drawer, Punch found the little skull. He held it in his hand and made faces at it. Why hadn't he thought to ask the old man about it last night?

Tom looked up from his nearly full suitcase and saw Punch's face. "Put it in your pocket," he suggested. "We can ask around in town to find out who bought one lately."

Punch didn't think they were going into town, but he dropped the skull into his pocket anyway. I'm going to put it in our hole at Hammock House, he decided.

Skeeter arrived at noon and they set out for the pirate's yard.

"Let's work fast," Punch said.

Tom and Skeeter nodded. "Hey, Skeeter?" asked Tom. "We've got something to show you. Get it out, Punch."

Punch dug in his pocket and held up the skull.

Skeeter burst into laughter. "You did find it then! I been wonderin'. Keep it for a souvenir. It goes on a key chain."

Punch frowned. "Why'd you do that? That was a really dirty trick."

"Was not either," Skeeter said virtuously. "I was tryin' to save your life and you didn't pay any mind to it a-tall. Stubborn Yankee."

"Know-it-all sixth-grader."

"Good. Glad we got it all straight," Skeeter replied matter-of-factly. "Look at that. Hammock House again. I can't believe we're back here." He stuck his tongue out at the house as he stepped over the fence into the backyard.

"This is terrible work," he groused. "Next summer we'll check out islands. Sand's a whole lot easier to dig."

"We really are coming back. Dad said so again this morning."

While they did their best to repair the appearance of Blackbeard's yard, they made plans for the next August — a time that sounded awfully far away. Skeeter promised to locate the island that the museum director thought was so promising, plus any others he could pinpoint through research at the library. "I'll be ready for y'all," he said.

Punch stomped sod into place and wondered if he'd feel the same about treasure hunting then. Will I still want to dig holes all the time on vacation?

I guess so, he decided. That dumb treasure is out there and I'm going to find it if it takes all six years till Skeeter goes to college.

When they couldn't make the yard look any better, they left. Punch glanced back at Hammock House as they walked away. Just a plain, two-story, two-chimney, white house. It just sits there, all innocent-like, he thought. Except we know better.

They were searching for the dolphins by midafternoon, under a scorching sun that burned down from a hard blue sky.

"I'm gonna try the back side a this island," Skeeter said after nearly an hour. "There's a little cove and sometimes I find 'em here, restin'."

"Yup!" Punch cried out as soon as they cruised into the quiet bay. "Isn't that Sweetheart?"

"Sure is. Y'all are gettin' good at this, Punch." Skeeter cut the engine and let the boat drift as he called to his favorite.

"Eee-eee!" squeaked Sweetheart, bucketing across the cove to greet them. "Eeeeee!" when she came up to the boat.

Punch reached out to pet the laughing, friendly mammal, and thought, this is it. My last chance.

"Skeeter," he said, "do you think she'd let me swim with her? I wouldn't touch her or anything, just sort of pretend to be another dolphin."

Skeeter dragged one hand through the hay on his head. "I guess. But don't try to be a dolphin. They play pretty rough sometimes. And if the school comes over, y'all get back in the boat."

Punch slipped overboard, all the while telling himself, stay cool, you can do this. It's just one little dolphin.

"EEEE!" Sweetheart squealed in his face, opening her mouth wide.

Punch felt himself tense up. Her head and mouth were huge when he was this close. He treaded water mechanically, appalled at what he had let himself in for. What if she decided to get rough?

"Grab on to her fin and go for a ride," coached Skeeter. "Hold tight and let go whenever you want, hear?"

"You'll probably drown," Tom said with a wicked grin.

That did it. Punch stretched up and took hold of Sweetheart's dorsal fin. "Let's go. You be a nice little dolphin, okay?"

Used to the hand on her fin, Sweetheart took off through the water. Punch lasted about four seconds before he was spun away by a powerful thrust of her flipper.

He surfaced to laughter. "Hey!" he called. "This is harder than it looks!"

"You gotta stay way behind that flipper," Skeeter said.

He did better the next time, letting go of the fin only when he ran out of air. He swam hard toward the surface, where he gasped for breath and tossed his head back. "Yahoo!" he whooped, when he could breathe.

"My turn," Tom begged. "Please? Before all the others swim over here."

"Be real careful," Skeeter cautioned. "Y'all are kinda big and Sweetheart's used to someone skinny like me or Punch."

Tom's time in the water was briefer because the rest of the dolphins decided to stir themselves and see what all the commotion was about. Still, he had one good circle around the boat before Skeeter waved him in.

"That's the coolest thing I ever did," Tom said, his chest heaving as he drew deep, ragged breaths.

All the dolphins ringed the boat then, seeking their share of petting and attention. Skeeter had brought a pail of small bait fish to feed them as a farewell present from Punch and Tom.

When the fish had been devoured and all the glistening gray bodies stroked and admired, the dolphins called to one another and headed for the inlet.

"Yessir," Punch said, pained at seeing them go, "purely amazin', they are."

Skeeter bobbed his head in pleasure at the subtle compliment. "Well, sun's goin' down. We better head on back. Sure was a quick two weeks. Now I gotta tote boards again till school starts."

Skeeter and his father came to the Wagners' house later that evening for a final visit and dessert.

"I can't believe it's our last night," said Punch's

mom. "The time just whizzed by. If we work at saving money, maybe we can stay longer next summer."

"We got the best life in the world here," Lanky said quietly. "I never wished I was anywhere else, long as I've lived."

"I understand that," said Punch's dad. "Lanky, did I hear that Rutherford Grace has decided he wants to go to college?"

Lanky nodded. "I promised him we'd study on it. Good theng he doesn't have to go tomorra."

"Yes, well, I don't want you to worry about it all these years. My university has an excellent biology department, and we also have scholarships. Even though I'm in another department, I could put in a word. Just thought I'd mention that before we leave."

"And we're all getting money from that old jewelry. Anytime now" — Punch turned to Skeeter — "you can open your own bank account."

Not all that we'd hoped, Punch thought, but it's a start, and he's only in sixth grade. Hoo-ee, talk about planning ahead. Still, the whole thing made him feel deep-down good — better than anything ever before.

Skeeter's eyes and face were bright. "Y'all are so nice. I — I don't know what to say."

"Hah!" Punch crowed. "Gotcha. We finally gotcha!"

"Just this once," Skeeter said lightly. "Mule-headed Yankee."